"LET ME GO!" SARA CRIED, STRUGGLING FUTILELY AGAINST HIS SUPERIOR STRENGTH...

"No! You run from my kisses but run to Christopher's arms like a wanton!" Lord Ramsey kissed her again with passionate intensity and Sara responded, answering his kisses with her own. Her arms twined around his neck and she felt the warmth of his strong hands caressing, molding her body to his.

Then with a shock she recalled herself, afraid, not of him but of her own passions. "Please! Let me go," she whispered, her eyes like sapphires in the moonlight.

Edward smiled sardonically. "Is that what you want? I think not!" He bent his head again and kissed her while his right hand expertly began to undo the buttons of her gown . . .

Second Chance at Love

REGENCY

AN ARTFUL LADY

SABINA CLARK

A JOVE BOOK

For Alessandra Francesca Willman
with love

First Jove edition published July 1981

First printing

"Second Chance at Love" and the butterfly emblem are trademarks
belonging to Jove Publications, Inc.

Printed in the United States of America

Jove books are published by Jove Publications, Inc.,
200 Madison Avenue, New York, N.Y. 10016

CHAPTER ONE

Sara was tickling her new kitten, Muse, under his furry white chin while her paint brushes soaked in turpentine before being cleaned and put away for the day. It was good to relax after a difficult sitting, and Sara was enjoying the romp with Muse. Her peace was broken by a disturbance, quite loud enough to penetrate from the foyer through the thick oak door to her studio. The kitten sprang from the lap of her black widow's gown as Sara rose.

"Madame cannot be disturbed for *any* reason!" Witherall was explaining in his most quelling voice. "Madame is conferring with her Muse!"

Sara repressed a chuckle at Witherall's appalling pun in order to hear the rejoinder. Out in the marble-tiled hall the little drama continued.

"Well, I am gratified to know that Madame Roche

1

communes on such a high level, but if you will persuade her to descend from so exalted a plane for a few moments it will be well worth her while."

"Alas, my lord," Witherall mourned, "it is not possible to disturb Madame when she is so engaged." Here, the butler gave a marvelous, if completely counterfeit, shudder. The visitor ignored both words and gestures, much to the butler's chagrin.

"I wish to take a very few minutes of your mistress's time. I am convinced at this moment that her time is more readily available than mine, so I must insist that you convey my regards and my intentions of having a few words with her!" Since the stranger was as well-muscled and athletic-appearing as he was assured, Witherall involuntarily took a step backward toward the studio door.

"My lord," the butler began again, his voice reflecting the ground he had lost in the face of the other man's uncompromising air of authority, but he was interrupted in mid-phrase.

"I will see Madame Roche, will you, nil you! So step aside and I will finish my business as quickly as possible."

Sara forestalled Witherall's inevitable defeat by pulling sharply on the bell cord. There was a brief exchange of words and then Witherall entered the studio. On the threshold he made an agonized bow. "You rang, madame?" he inquired, face twisted with bogus fear. Deftly closing the door behind him, he lifted a brow in response to the merry twinkle in Sara's eyes.

"Witherall, you old rogue! I should send you back to that obscure repertory company immediately, if you weren't so vastly entertaining. Make sure that odious man, whoever he may be, thinks that I beat you unmercifully!"

"As you should, indeed, madame!" responded the actor-cum-butler in his suavest accents before lapsing into one of his more familiar cadences with a laugh. "Lor', you shoulda seen th' gentry mort's fiz when I told 'im you was conversin' with yer Muse! Right good shade of ruddy he got."

Stifling a giggle, Sara placed finger to lips and signaled for softer voices. "So," she chortled, "this most importunate gentleman thinks his time is more valuable than mine? You may tell him that I will give him five minutes of *my* precious time . . . if he will only wait fifteen of his, until I am done with my . . . er . . . meditations. That should make him either angry enough to send him packing, or annoy him at least as much as his rudeness has annoyed me!" she laughed.

Witherall grinned, then attempted to compose himself once more into the exquisitely supercilious servant he presented to callers at Madame Roche's house in Green Dolphin Street.

"Yes, madame. As you wish," he intoned.

With a flourish, he removed himself from the room. And he delivered his mistress's message well, judging by the curt, angry-sounding response from the stranger.

Despite her nine-and-twenty years, Sara was hard put to keep from peering through the keyhole like a schoolgirl to watch the fireworks she felt were sure to explode over Witherall's head. To her intense surprise, disappointment even, there was no further outburst from the gentleman in the foyer. There were only the sounds of boots prowling back and forth across the tiled floor and occasional mutters which, though muffled by the oak door, sounded suspiciously as though they were produced from between gnashed teeth.

Sara passed the fifteen minutes by cleaning her brushes and setting a clean pad of sketching paper on the tall easel which stood between herself and the door. She covered her black dress with a long muslin apron. When the alotted time was up, Witherall entered the studio again. In the unconventional form his mistress had decreed for all prospective clients, he announced, "The gentleman, madame." But here he added something special, "The gentleman who was waiting."

The butler stepped aside to reveal a tall and quite devastatingly handsome man who moved into the room with an easy grace despite his shock at the unorthodox method of introduction employed by Witherall. The gentleman's eyes searched the room, which appeared empty since Sara was well hidden behind her easel. Then, as he glanced about, Sara emerged in her muslin apron. His mind registered surprise that this young, tiny woman with a slightly misty gaze in her blue-grey eyes was the same woman who had made him cool his heels for a quarter hour and evidently terrorized her butler.

Sara, on the other hand, was unprepared for the tall, very elegantly attired stranger who entered. He was quite the most handsome man she had ever seen. For just an instant before her wits returned and the artist superseded the woman, she found herself wishing she had not put on the paint-stained apron.

"Your servant," the tall man began, "is indeed an original! My name, Madame Roche, is..."

His declaration and bow were abruptly arrested by Sara's outthrust hand. "Pray, do not make your name known to me! It is one of my rules! I have no wish to influence my paintings by such dismissible vagaries as name, rank, fortune or gossip."

The gentleman paused, then completed his bow and made as if to speak, but Sara again forestalled him, looking over his face and trim figure.

"There is no need to speak at this time," she said. "I wish to immerse myself in visual impressions at the first meeting. Of course, you've come to have your portrait done." She pointed to an old, faded tapestry-covered arm-chair. "Sit there," she commanded.

The stranger, cautious as in the presence of one obviously disordered in mind, did as he was bid. A glint of humor appeared in his eyes, which with a twitch of his mobile mouth, helped to counteract the arrogance of his fine high-bridged nose. He gave himself up to the moment, sat in the old chair, folded his hands and gave Sara his complete attention as he waited expectantly to see what further surprises this meeting had in store for him.

Slowly, Sara walked around the chair, examining the gentleman's face and figure from all angles. For a man more accustomed to be on the delivering end of such appraising looks, he appeared to tolerate the procedure quite comfortably at first, although the intentness of Sara's gaze as she looked into his eyes gave him an inner qualm. He felt she was looking into his very soul and hoped there was nothing there to alarm her too drastically.

Her gaze intent—as much due to her slight nearsightedness as to her deep concentration—Sara remained oblivious to any stray thoughts in which the stranger engaged.

"Yes," she mused aloud. "A good face. Strong and determined, but honest overall. A bit self-willed and indulgent, perhaps." The gentleman lifted one eyebrow in sardonic amusement. "Yes," she repeated, "good planes. And the nose prevents it from being too pretty." At this the stranger gave a slight start, partly because the term "pretty" was applied to his face, which had seen hardship and war in the Pyrenees, and partly because of pique at having his face referred to as "it"!

Sara continued her inspection. "That tilt to the eyebrows does give a rather wicked look."

The stranger merely cocked one of those brows while continuing to sit quietly until she reached out a hand and grasped his chin in a businesslike manner. She firmly turned his head up and to the right. "Begging your pardon, ma'am!" Indignation set gold lights afire in the man's dark eyes.

"Really!" Sara responded. "If you want me to do your portrait, you must get used to me adjusting the angles of the pose. And," she continued since he seemed on the verge of speech, "you must not talk when I am working unless I give you leave. It wrecks my concentration and completely destroys the lines!" Her artist's eye again noted the sudden warm amber illumination that filled his irises.

"Very well. I will do your portrait," Sara sighed, "though I am certainly busy enough without another commission. At first," she went on, almost to herself, "I thought your features too handsome, too regular. However, there is a fierceness about the eyes and nose and jaw that intrigues me." Her voice trailed off as she rummaged through the compartments of her mind, trying to decide how she might capture in oils those golden sparks the gentleman's eyes radiated at times. As she turned away, the kitten stalked and attacked the hem of her long skirt. "No, Muse. Go play with your yarn ball. I shall need to think quietly for a while."

With a vague wave of her hand and an absentminded statement that she would expect him Tuesday-a-week at two o'clock in the afternoon, Sara dismissed the stranger. The gentleman bowed to her back and exited with a wry smile. In a short time he was out in the late-afternoon sunlight, and in a smiliar state of somnambulism to Sara's, but for far different reasons.

He was very nearly certain that this mere slip of a woman, artist or no, this impudent and entertaining and original woman, had actually kept him, Edward, sixth Earl of Ramsey, quietly kicking his heels while she played with her *cat!* Well, today he admitted to himself, the honors were all to Madame Roche, but Tuesday next would be a different story. He would have to cry off his shopping expedition with Lady Pamela, for he definitely planned to keep his appointment for the sitting. This last thought brought him up short, and the Earl dashed the hopes of two lovely young ladies strolling with their maids by not only failing to acknowledge them, but by giving every evidence that they were as invisible as the very air.

Indeed, the Earl had been so bemused it was only the thought of Lady Pamela which caused him to remember that he had totally subverted the mission on which he'd been sent. Lady Pamela had charged him to convince the unattainable and eccentric Madame Roche, whose portraits were all the rage, to execute a likeness of her. Only a Madame Roche portrait would do for the beautiful and willful Lady Pamela Kennerly, the reigning Incomparable . . . and the affianced wife of the Sixth Earl of Ramsey. And now it was he, instead, who was to sit for the charming—and mysterious—lady portraitist!

CHAPTER TWO

In the snug brick house on Green Dolphin Street, Sara composed herself for the final appointment of the day. So absorbed had she been in planning the coming sitting for "the gentleman who waited," that it had been difficult to resist postponing the visit from the next patron. After nearly two years of purposefully donning invisible armor against involvement with anyone except those in her own small, private world, Sara was beginning to feel a growing interest in something other than her painting and in people other than those in her immediate circle. For the first time since her reckless husband's death in a duel and the ensuing scandal, Sara felt stirrings of curiosity about the characters and lives of the people whose likenesses she captured so superbly.

Her mind conjured up an image of the Earl of Ramsey.

With no clue to his real identity other than his person and elegant tailoring, she let her thoughts drift, trying to fit him into some pattern. The secret of Sara's success lay not only in her faultless technique, but also in her fertile imagination. By not knowing the true identities of her subjects, she was able to assess their characters without distraction and to translate this assessment to the mood of each portrait. Of course, the patrons did not know this little stratagem. Sara laughed aloud thinking of the reaction the formidable Mrs. Buller-Throcton would sustain if she ever dreamed that the swirling mauve-to-angry-red clouds haloing her portrait were a reflection of Sara's perception of the Society matron as a spiritual descendant of Lady MacBeth! And Lord Musgrave's fearless and flint-eyed representation had been Sara's rendering of a Corsican pirate in Regency dress!

This new gentleman, Sara thought, was not a pirate. An adventurer perhaps? While he was unmistakably a gentleman of the first stare, there was something intriguing about his economical but controlled movements, a certain graceful strength that conveyed a similarity to the smooth rippling walk of a panther.

A discreet tap recalled Sara to her surroundings. Witherall opened the studio door and announced coolly, "The gentleman from America, madame!"

Sara met her last visitor of the day, a rather lean, blond gentleman with graying temples and a smile that could more aptly be called a grin. His face and hands were tanned and weathered, and there were fine lines at the corners of his eyes that might have come from staring across long distances in sunlight. More probably, Sara thought, they resulted from the frequent laughter that accompanies a naturally sunny disposition.

"Howdy-do, ma'am," the gentleman began. "You have a very pleasant place here."

"How do you do," Sara responded, unable to keep an answering smile from her lips.

"Now that's a sight better," the American said. "I was in a terrible quake out there, make you no mind about it. Why, from all I'd heard about you, I was sure you would be seven feet tall and have lightning bolts blazing from your eyes!"

"Oh, no!" gasped Sara, chuckling a bit. "Is my reputation really so fearful? I am delighted, for it can only enhance my privacy!"

To this the gentleman nodded and smiled. "I am sure, ma'am, that you must have a great need for privacy, for any lady as pleasing to the eye as yourself must have to barricade the doors!"

At this Sara blushed. She was astonished that, despite the maturity she'd attained, she could still respond like a schoolroom chit to a compliment. The American gentleman, misinterpreting the flush, apologized, adding that his "New World manners were perhaps a bit too forward."

"Pray make yourself easy on that score, sir," Sara answered, "for manners as amiable as yours must be sure to please even the most querulous old dowager."

The gentleman bowed in acknowledgment and Sara invited him to be seated as Witherall entered with a cut-glass decanter and two glasses on a silver tray. The butler served the port and withdrew silently in his best imitation of a stiff and proper manservant.

The tall man gave a contented sigh. "I cannot tell you, ma'am," he said, "how pleasant it is to sit and talk a while with a lady. Since my wife died, I've spent a lot of time with my family, but all my social contacts seem to be with other men engaged in shipping as I am." Here he paused apologetically and quickly added, "I'm sorry, ma'am, for I did understand that it is distracting to your work to know the background of those who commission your portraits!"

Sara placed him at ease, stating that as she knew little of shipping or Americans, his small slip of tongue could do no harm.

"Tell me," she continued, "who is to be the subject of the portrait? I am convinced it is not you."

"No indeed!" laughed the American, who became suddenly very earnest as he continued. "It is my daughter, Janie. I don't really know quite how to explain... Her mother was just the most beautiful little thing you ever did see. A mite of a woman with golden ringlets, eyes the color of cornflowers, skin that would make a magnolia hang its head in despair." He paused, abstracted.

Touched, Sara sat quietly while the gentleman was lost in reverie for a few moments. "Well, I guess, m'am, I don't have to say more to *you* on the subject," he added with a sympathetic look at Sara's widow's garb.

Sara nodded, an understanding smile curving her lips. "Your daughter, I gather, does not favor her late mother?"

"That's exactly right!" the American answered. "Janie takes after her old dad. She's tall and slim and brown and has hazel eyes like me. Now don't get me wrong, Janie is a real beauty, but..." Again he stopped, groping for words to explain.

"But your daughter doesn't agree because her ideal of beauty is tiny and golden."

"Yes!" exclaimed the gentleman. "I knew you would understand from the moment I first saw one of your portraits. It was of Mr. Soloman McDonald. When I saw how you had seen past his crusty exterior to the warmth and gentleness beneath, I was sure you would be able to make Janie see herself as she truly is in all her sweet loveliness." As he said this, he rose and walked a few paces. He hesitated a moment, then made a decision. "The world I live in is new and exciting and filled with young energy. We're making a country from wilderness, and we have to make up the rules as best we can as we go along. If Janie had been brought up in England as her mother was, she would have a very different life. Her friends would call her 'Miss Ames' or 'Jeanette,' not 'Janie' as they all do in Virginia. She'd never have gone out for a walk without a parasol to shade her from the sun and without an abigail or groom in attendance. Instead, she's grown up like an Indian maid, playing hide and seek in the woods, and running or riding through the fields like a nymph.

"Not," he said quickly, "to give you any false idea! I must say Janie is a perfect lady and knows just what is so and what ain't quite the thing. Still there are no young ladies—indeed, few women—near our estate, for her to talk with. She's grown up with my neighbor's two sons and a few other young fellows as her companions."

He turned and took a few steps around the room. Sara watched him with a smile on her lips. She was charmed by the man's amazing candor with a perfect stranger. Even though she had heard that Americans were frank people who did not stand on ceremony, she was unprepared for his ease of manner and found herself warming to him against her will.

"Am I right in guessing that there is, perhaps, a possible suitor who is the cause of your concern?" Sara ventured.

"Exactly so, ma'am!" the American acknowledged with a relieved sigh. "Somehow I felt the moment I saw you that you were the kind of woman a man could talk to comfortably without a lot of roundaboutation." He eased himself into the chair next to Sara's and leaned forward with an earnest look on his pleasant face.

"I've known Paul MacAllister from the day he was born. In fact, his father and I were inseparable as boys and are still close. Mrs. MacAllister was taken off by the typhoid within two weeks of my wife, and the loss of their mothers was another link between our children."

"It would seem to be a most unexceptionable match, sir, provided of course, your daughter is of the same mind as the young man?" Sara queried politely.

"That is just it, ma'am. Young Paul vows that Janie is the only woman he'll ever marry, and Janie has worshiped him from the time she was able to toddle after him."

"Ah," said Sara. "I'm beginning to understand. Your daughter has known this young man all her life and is ready to settle down with him. You, however, would be more content if she had seen something of the world before coming to such an important decision."

"My dear ma'am," the gentleman replied in admiration, "you are as wise as you are charming! That is exactly the quandary I've found myself in. On one hand I couldn't hope for a more considerate and faithful husband for Janie. On the other, I feel I owe it to her to see that she has a taste of Society before she throws her cap over the windmill for what may be, after all, a schoolgirl crush!"

"And if after all is said and done, your daughter still prefers the Virginian?"

"Why, then I would be the happiest man in the world! But I would not want to influence Janie's decision by my wishes."

Sara could not conceal a smile at the affection the man had for his daughter and felt that it must be mutual. "What a fortunate young lady your daughter is, sir, to have a father to value her at her true worth."

"Then you will accept the commission for her portrait?"

"I am sure she must be every bit as amiable as her parent, and I will look forward to meeting her."

"Ma'am, I am deeply in your debt. In fact I find it impossible to find words to express my gratitude."

"No, sir! You are not in my debt until I have finished the painting," Sar said, a mischievous twinkle in her eyes.

"And you may not feel such gratitude, for my fees are shockingly dear!"

"Well, I only know your portraits are the most wonderful I've ever seen, and my daughter says you are all the kick! If your portrait does for my Janie what I think it will, it would be worth every cent I have!"

"A fond father indeed!" Sara murmured, and the meeting was concluded with an agreement for a preliminary sitting on the approaching Tuesday at the highly unfashionable hour of ten o'clock. As Witherall ushered the American out, Sara smiled to herself. After all, this had been an interesting day. A *most* interesting day! She wandered over to the tall French windows that led out to the charming walled garden, her favorite retreat in good weather. Mellowed rose brick walls contrasted pleasantly with the varying shades of green of the flowering plants and espaliered fruit trees. She scooped up her kitten who was ferociously attacking a tiny twig and carried him over to the bench under the grape arbor. She held his furry little body tenderly and patted his head while he purred in contentment. Her thoughts drifted back to her two visitors. They were both gentlemen, both obviously men of means and both exceedingly personable. There, the similarity ended.

The American, it was clear, was a good-humored and easygoing man, who would take pains to put others at ease. And, though perhaps on the thin side, he had the look of a wiry, strong man who spent a great deal of time in the out-of-doors. Sara wondered what the Society matrons would make of him. She was inclined to think that any qualms they had respecting his disregard for the conventional forms would be outweighed by his charm *and* his undoubted fortune!

The other gentleman, Sara had recognized, was a member of the *ton*. He had the air of a man who finds himself equal to any social situation and the confidence that comes of good breeding. The attire of "the gentleman who waited" was correct to a shade, and Sara was not taken in by the deceptively simple cut of his coat—only Weston or Stultz could achieve the perfection of fit that followed every contour without the smallest wrinkle or bulge. He had a very attractive smile, and Sara thought she had perceived a merry glint in his eye one or more times. She wasn't deceived, though. His lips would thin out to a stern line and those unusual eyes would flash like lightning if his temper were aroused. Sara's uncanny ability to accurately assess a person's temperament on brief acquaintance had informed her that this was a man who was used to having things his own way. He was not someone to cross lightly!

Muse decided at this time to take a nip at Sara's hand, interrupting her train of thought. With a shake of her finger at the kitten, and a mental shake at herself, Sara dismissed both men from her thoughts.

Having changed into a dove-colored dress with black banding and redressed her thick ash-brown hair. Sara went along the small passageway outside her own bedchamber and tapped at the second-from-last doorway. A wan voice invited her into a room with a greater quantity of furniture than the rest of the house boasted. The room was quite large, having been originally two small rooms which had been knocked together. A huge old four-posted bed was placed in the center of the far wall and would have dominated the space except for the fact that the bed hangings, draperies, cushions and wallpaper were all in a smothering pattern of large pink roses the size of cabbages. The whole effect was to make the figure reclining against the many pillows and bolsters on the oversized couch before the fireplace seem small and frail as a porcelain figurine. Yet

again Sara was amazed at the incredible effect the decor
had of altering perspective. Even her well-trained eye re-
corded the bundled woman as one of tiny proportions,
when she knew very well that Aunt Gussie topped her by
at least a head!

"Good evening, Aunt," Sara said.

"Oh, my! Is it time for dinner already? Why I have just
now gotten settled for my nap." The older woman sighed.

Sara could not help but smile for she had been able to
hear her aunt snoring regularly all of the past two hours
while she went over household accounts. Aunt Augusta
was so kind and so dear, though, that Sara did not grudge
her recent flirtation with invalidism. Like all her aunt's
rather theatrical, but harmless fancies, this latest fad of
being on death's doorstep could not last long. Gussie had
a lively intelligence and curiosity. A handsome woman of
only forty-odd, she would soon be bored with the life of
an invalid. With a sigh Sara thanked her stars that Aunt
Gussie had finally gotten over her previous pose of being
a serious and determined poetess. She had endured two
entire months of poetry readings with her aunt's cronies,
drinking tea or orgeat while being regaled with immortal
bits of rhyme such as Gussie's personal favorite, "Ode to
a Butterchurn." Since Gussie's enthusiasms usually in-
convenienced only herself, Sara had regarded this episode
very unhappily indeed.

"I've told Witherall that we will dine in your solar,
Aunt, for I fear the fire is too warm here for you." They
both knew that Gussie's flushed face and slightly glassy
eyes were from the multitude of shawls and lap rugs heaped
around her rather than the barely flickering fire. The adjoining sitting room had become Gussie's "solar" during
her days of "living history," when, for all intents and
purposes, she was a Medieval Lady. This fad like several
others had passed quickly, but the sobriquet had clung to

the cheerful room with its large windows overlooking the small walled garden.

Gussie rose languorously from the couch, but ruined the effect by striding to her wardrobe and flinging the heavy door open with a casual flick of the wrist. She rummaged around for a few minutes, pulling out a variety of luxurious dressing gowns. She hesitated. A deep maroon silk accented her very white skin and guinea-gold curls. An aquamarine silk with a froth of lace cascading down at neckline and sleeves, exactly matched the color of her eyes.

Sara watched in affectionate amusement the battle between drama and vanity. Vanity carried the day, and Gussie donned the aquamarine confection.

"You look splendid, Aunt!"

"Oh, dear!" Gussie exclaimed in dismay. "Do you really think so?" She looked as though her allegiance to the blue-green gown was wavering.

"For a woman who has just risen from her sick bed!" Sara amended. Mollified, Gussie took her arm and the two women proceeded to the solar.

Sara solicitously arranged a pillow behind Gussie and once comfortably settled, the ladies indulged in their ritual of a glass of sherry before dinner. The setting sun illuminated the pleasant room, gilding the alcove with its small chairs and table where Witherall was busily setting out the covers for their meal.

Over a dinner of lamb with new potatoes and green peas, removed with a jelly tart and custards, the two ladies discussed the events of the day. Only when she was retiring did Gussie reflect that they had spent much time speculating about the daughter of the gentleman from America, less time on that gentleman himself and, oddly enough, hardly any on "the gentleman who waited." A small frown briefly puckered Gussie's brow. However, the sudden discovery of two more audacious gray hairs among her curly golden locks soon distracted her for the rest of the evening.

Alone in her room, Sara did something she hadn't done since her husband was killed two years before—she thought about the future. Not just tomorrow or the next week, but about the months and even years ahead. Jerome had died so senselessly . . . and shamefully. Sara had been torn by grief, by anger, by regret—and by the very real fear of how to provide a home for herself and his widowed aunt.

Two years ago, even one year ago, she thought, having a roof over their heads and food on the table was more than she hoped for. Now even being successful . . . but Sara could not complete the thought. She longed for something she could not identify. She stared at the stars, but they were cold and bright and far away, offering no comfort.

"Ah, Jerome!" Sara said aloud, sighing softly. Her thoughts flew back to the first time she had seen him. To the little girl of ten years of age, a boy of ten and three was a magical, wondrous creature, infinitely worthy of her unquestioning adoration.

Sara was crying because the Albertson twins had thrown her rag doll into the crotch of a gnarled oak tree, far too high for her short little legs to climb. Suddenly, a lordly young boy appeared through the hedge where he was stalking rabbits, wanting to know "what all the caterwauling was about."

Sara pointed to the high branch where her doll was sprawled limply up against the main trunk. The young man ordered her to cut her infernal noise and hold his soft-tipped bow and arrow set while he rescued her "baby."

The young man, of course, was Jerome Roche, the orphaned son of Mrs. Elston's sister, of a distinguished but impecunious line stretching back to the Battle of Hastings. Indeed Jerome rescued Sara's rag doll, but managed to fall on his way down, breaking his leg and knocking himself senseless. Sara was his willing slave that summer, running errands, reading stories, sketching pictures and anything else she could think of to divert her hero during the slow summer days of his convalescence. Over the years this became the pattern of their relationship. Jerome, the knight errant, slaying dragons and rescuing fair damsels, even if they were only rag dolls, and Sara, the Lady-in-the-Tower, waiting for her hero to return, bandaging his wounds, soothing his hurts and openly adoring him, until a new adventure called him away from her side. Jerome, the impractical idealist. Sara, the realist.

If Jerome's sense of idealism had never let him forgive himself—*or* Sara— for the fact that he had taken her just before they became man and wife, still they had dealt well together. How often Sara had sighed and pined because she couldn't come up with any argument that would cause Jerome to be the least lenient about their lapse from propriety. No matter they were young and passionate. No matter the unusual circumstances that brought them together and into each other's arms. And it was his very lack of forgiveness on this subject that had caused his death.

Long after they'd wed, when her cousin Alfred had made a disparaging remark about her purity before marriage, an enraged Jerome had called him out. They'd both died from the wounds they inflicted on one another. Grief was hard enough for Sara to bear without the gossip, the ugly ripples of gossip about her and the duel. How much the *ton* seemed to relish the sensationalism drawn from events Sara could see only as tragic. She would wonder always how severely she would have been ostracized had she not voluntarily withdrawn from Society. But, then, it hadn't been *voluntary* really. There was the problem of funds—or rather lack of them. She had been forced to immerse herself in painting, to push her talent and reputation in directions that would provide a home for Gussie and herself, and, of course, the means of running it.

At last Sara crawled into bed. It was huge and empty, the sheets chill. Unwilling to acknowledge the ache in her loins, she tossed and turned restlessly until a combination of sheer will power and genuine tiredness finally eased her into a deep slumber. Oddly, she dreamed not of Jerome, but of a panther with amber eyes.

While Sara and Gussie lay deep in dreams, the Earl of Ramsey was excusing himself to his hostess and hieing himself off to his club to spend the remainder of the night among his intimates. He stopped en route at his town house and changed into clothing a shade less formal, then joined his friends for a light repast and a game of cards.

Young Binghampton, Lord Kennerly's son and heir, hailed the Earl cheerfully as he entered the club. "I say, Ramsey, you made good your escape just as you said. Why, I have lost a monkey to John Ketcham over you; I was positive Mama and 'the Queen' would keep you dancing attendance till fish grew fur."

"More shame to you, then," Ramsey rejoined. "Surely my reputation for punctual civility must have made you realize the folly of your wager!"

"Enough!" Bing laughed. "I should have known your cool head would see you through. Not to mention your quelling ways!"

"Why? Do you really think me as toplofty was that? I should have you know this very day I received the setdown of setdowns! And by a woman no higher than my shoulder at that!"

"The woman you can't handle, be she quality or light-skirt, has not been born yet," his friend replied.

"I assure 'tis God's truth," the Earl said and recounted the unusual half hour he had spent at the studio of the formidable Madame Roche.

"What!" Bing exclaimed. "You did not arrange for Pamela's portrait! Why she has been bragging to all her bosom beaux that she is to have her wedding portrait by the mysterious Madame Roche. How comes it that you are arrived here intact, without any sign of wounds or blood loss?"

"Have done!" Ramsey responded with a trace of ice in his voice. Only slightly abashed, his friend desisted with the retort that he had known his own sister for eighteen years, while Ramsey had known her a scant three months.

The talk turned to other subjects, a game of cards was gotten up. The friends parted amicably in those small hours of morning when the night had not yet given up its reign, but was beginning to be challenged by the prelight heralding dawn.

With a yawn, the Earl prepared for bed, his thoughts turning once again to his visit to Madame Sara Roche's home in Green Dolphin Street. He was both amused and chagrined by the whole episode and vowed to himself that he would wield the upper hand at their next meeting.

As he drifted off to sleep, he dreamed, not of panthers, but of small white kittens. With claws.

CHAPTER THREE

Sara was mixing paints early in the morning when Witherall unceremoniously poked his head through the doorway.

"Oh," Sara exclaimed, taking in the neat dark suit, pince-nez and new wig that Witherall sported in place of his usual butler's livery. "I collect you are *Witherspoon*, my man of business, today!"

"Just so, madame," Witherall responded in plumy tones.

"What an excellent wig," she remarked. "Why, if I didn't know you, I wouldn't dream that was not your very own hair."

"Madame is too kind," Witherall responded with mock severity, ducking quickly back through the doorway.

Sara chuckled. Witherall was something of a mystery,

though a delightful and valued one! He'd appeared on Sara's doorstep a few days after the duel in which Jerome had been killed, with a note from Jerome and an explanation that he'd promised her husband he would look after "the wife and aunt in event of unfortunate circumstances."

Witherall had been with Sara and Augusta ever since. They knew little about him, except that he believed Jerome had saved his life . . . and that he'd been an actor. In a rare lapse, Witherall had confided he was London-born and -bred and had toured the provinces with an obscure drama troupe. Given free rein in Sara's easygoing household, his creativity—theatrical to be sure, but convincing nonetheless—had given birth to the alter egos of "Witherspoon," "Witherbee," "Witherly" and a host of fleeting minor characters. He seemed never to be bored with any of his roles, and his loyalty to the two women was without question.

Sara hummed as she worked. She reserved every morning and all day Monday for herself. Instead of shopping or visiting or occupying herself with any of the usual activities of a woman of her age and station, she experimented with mixing colors and with obtaining unusual effects in the application of her oils. Today she was trying to find ways of capturing the light "that man" had in his eyes. The gentleman-who-waited had become "that man!" sometime during the early hours when her thoughts kept flying back to him as if drawn by a magnet. It made her unwarrantedly out of sorts.

Throughout the morning, Sara heard the sounds of voices from the small parlor across the hall where Witherall conducted business relating to payment for the portraits. She smiled to herself thinking of his enjoyment in creating and acting out the parts of various servants. Once Sara had tried to dissuade him, but dire mumblings about "not fittin' dealin's fer ha' lidy" and his general air of gloom had made her retreat from this stand. Her only apprehension was that he might try his hand at nursemaid or parlor maid, and and that, she thought, would be beyond anything. She never voiced this aloud for fear she would set the idea in Witherall's mind . . . with unfortunate consequences to all.

The opening and closing of doors in the entryway and a voice of a certain timbre made Sara come to with a start. She realized she had been straining her ears for some time, hoping to catch that distinctive voice.

She went to the door and carefully, near-sightedly, peered through the large brass keyhole. Her field of vision was obscured by blue surperfine. She shifted the angle of her vision and was appalled to see the gentleman with the golden-amber eyes looking straight at the door, perhaps straight at the keyhole. While she remained frozen for an awful moment, he raised the small quizzing glass that hung at his waist with one gold watch fob, and appeared to stare right back at her.

Sara stood up so abruptly that she bumped a small candle table, knocking a china shepherdess to the floor where it shattered into a hundred pieces. After the total silence that followed, Sara flushed as the gentleman re- marked to Witherall, "What a unique door handle and plate." A few seconds later, another satisfying sound of breaking china reached his ears.

Witherall, to whom the remark ostensibly had been addressed, looked at the very plain, very ordinary fittings on the door with a bewildered air.

While Sara was left to fume in mortification behind her studio door, and Witherall was left to puzzle the strange ways of the Gentry, the Earl went down the front steps with a very satisfied expression. To an old dowager passing by with her companion, it sounded as if he said softly, "Second round to me!"

Of course after that episode, Tuesday arrived much too soon for Sara's comfort. While she looked forward to meeting the daughter of the American gentleman, she was not optimistic about her later appointment. In the usual way of things, no gentleman of quality would embarrass a lady by remarking on her propensity for peeping through keyholes. Still, Sara feared she could not depend on it. She would just have to carry it off as if the whole incident had never occurred.

A polite tap on the studio door heralded her first appointment. Witherall threw open the door announcing the arrival of "the gentleman from America and the Goddess Diana."

Her visitor of the past week entered with an enchanting girl on his arm. Witherall's choice of words brought a rosy blush to her cheeks which served as a lovely counterpoint to her sun-touched skin and glowing dark hair. Her hazel eyes, fringed with dark lashes, stood out startlingly against her honey-toned skin.

Why, Sara thought, she *is* a beauty! No milk-white English miss would allow herself to become darkened from the sun, but if this young lady could but carry her looks off with an air of confidence, she would take London by storm!

Greetings were exchanged. Sara turned to the young woman. "Witherall's forthright ways must not embarrass you, my dear, for he is right. You look as if you would be as much at home in the forests with the wild deer eating from your hand as in a drawing room."

"Much more at home, to be sure, ma'am, for I have spent vast amounts of my time running free in the woods of Virginia like a hoyden," the girl answered smilingly.

Yes, Sara thought, the daughter shared the same easy manners and address as her father. She would charm the young bucks and probably enrage all the scheming mamas of hopeful daughters.

The three chatted for a while and then the American

excused himself so the sitting could begin, promising to return in two hours to collect his daughter.

For once Sara relaxed her rule and encouraged conversation while she sketched. She hoped to put the young woman at ease; she also felt a great friendliness for the girl so far from home. Time flew, and when the American gentleman returned, he was immensely pleased to find Sara and Janie engrossed in spirited conversation. He glanced admiringly at Sara's sparkling eyes and quick, skillful fingers dancing across the sheets of sketch paper and wondered what had occurred to make such a desirable woman retreat from Society.

Father and daughter accepted eagerly Sara's invitation to stay for a light meal. They'd scarcely been served when Witherall announced a gentleman in the front hall was insisting he had an appointment for a sitting, that Madame Roche was late, and he would see her on the instant.

"Show him in," Sara replied in some consternation. She had looked forward to meeting the "gentleman who waited" with no little trepidation and was amazed she had been so caught up with her new acquaintances that she had put him completely out of mind.

In a few moments Witherall ushered the Earl in. Sara's apparent confusion made it clear she had forgotten her second sitting of the day. The American attempted to smooth things over with polite conversation. His trivial, but innocent comments seemed to incense the new arrival whose brow darkened and whose eyes seemed unusually golden. Since the Earl declined to partake of the nuncheon and sat staring out the window unless directly addressed, the little party broke up rather quickly.

When the Americans took their leave, Sara and the Earl went directly to the studio. She picked up the sketches she had done of Janie and turned to put them away, but found her way blocked. The Earl put out his arms to steady her, and Sara almost jumped at the feel of his hard hands on her shoulders. The warmth of his hands and the sudden spark she saw in his eyes made her feel confused and strangely awkward. For a long second they regarded each other, then at the same time both stepped back, dropping their arms to their sides.

The sketch sheets were scattered around their feet, and in the few moments it took to retrieve them Sara recovered herself. She directed the gentleman to be seated. In her anxiety to appear controlled and at ease she dropped her charcoal stick, but quickly picked it up before he could rise to his feet. She could have sworn he was laughing secretly at her. She walked directly behind his chair and began to draw.

"What? Are you going to do my portrait only from the back?"

"I always begin with the back of the head," Sara fabricated. The gentleman did not respond, but his strong shoulders shook suspiciously. Goaded, Sara continued. "You can tell a great deal about a person's character from the back of his head." Since there was no response to this, she sketched furiously for ten minutes until she had no choice but to change her position.

She chose next to work on the profile so she could avoid his eyes a while longer. It was impossible, however, to ignore the slight twitch of his mouth which seemed likely to erupt in a mischievous smile at the slightest provocation. After a few moments she became engrossed in catching a certain line of cheekbone and jaw, completely forgetting her uncustomary self-consciousness. In deep concentration she continued walking around him and sketching quickly. She set her larger pad on the easel and more slowly began to work on a drawing of his face.

The Earl, realizing Sara was rapt in a world of her own, took this time to admire her pretty face and neat figure.

Not that her looks were in the accepted mode. Her hair was smooth and dark while the ideal for an accepted beauty was all gold ringlets and dimples. Her eyes beneath dark winged brows had the soft blue-gray glow of the Celts instead of the currently much admired robin's-egg hue.

Altogether, the Earl mused, Madame Roche was a very cozy armful of woman indeed! That the American had come to the same conclusion, he was sure, for he had seen the warm looks bestowed on Sara. Although the daughter was quite unexceptional, the Earl discovered he had taken an unreasoning—but nevertheless definite—dislike to the father. He glared across the room and was startled to see Sara looking at him in surprise.

"Are you uncomfortable, sir?" she inquired. "Perhaps you would like to take a turn about the room...or the garden," she amended as the Earl rose to his feet and made as if to come forward.

"If you will accompany me, madame," he answered with a little bow. "Surely a little sunshine and fresh air would be delightful after your labors."

Quickly, Sara put down her materials and cleansed her hands in the ewer and basin set kept in readiness on the sideboard. She led the way to the tall double doors that opened to the small walled garden where delphiniums and columbines bowed to damask roses. He followed her along the flagstone path and past a topiary pear tree.

"A lovely setting!" the Earl exclaimed, stopping himself just short of saying "for such a lovely jewel," as he would have to any other beautiful woman of his acquaintance. Somehow he did not think this woman would approve of flowery phrases from a man who was not her lover. Did she have a lover, he wondered. Certainly she was too much of a woman to be content to remain unattached, and that would of course explain her retirement from the social scene.

They took seats beneath the grape arbor.

"I understand, madame, that you are cousin to my friend, Maria Sefton. How is it I have not made your acquaintance before?" He hoped he had not betrayed the fact he had made inquiries concerning her.

"Sir, you must know that I am a widow and live with my late husband's aunt who is also a widow. We are quite content to live in a quiet way; and I have my painting to occupy me."

"And your aunt," he ventured, "does she occupy herself with painting also?"

"No, my aunt does not paint!" She sat in silence, thinking of how Gussie had liked to entertain, and then drew in her breath in sharp surprise. In her own blind desire—and need—to escape from Society, she had never stopped to question whether the retired life suited Gussie. A stricken look came to her face. How *could* she have been so selfish?

"Forgive me," the Earl said. "I fear I have offended you. Would you like to return to the studio?"

"If you don't mind," Sara responded in a choked voice. "I would prefer to continue at another time."

The Earl took his leave, wondering what had made her so overset, then sad. And he cursed himself under his breath as he descended the front steps, fearing he might have been the cause. He had fought an incredible urge to sweep Sara into his arms and comfort her. He shook himself. It was indeed time he married when he wanted to make love to a woman with whom he was scarcely acquainted. He would speak to Lady Pamela about setting a date for the wedding as soon as possible.

Sara, meanwhile, could not work, not even straighten the cluttered studio. She was castigating herself about her aunt Augusta. How selfish she had been in never thinking deeply of the effect of her withdrawal from Society on the older woman. And she owed Gussie so much better than that. Whatever would she and Jerome have done without the wonderful woman? Aunt Gussie had, truly, saved them both, and on this reflection, Sara's thoughts winged to the past.

In the summer of her sixteenth year, she'd bloomed like a rose. Jerome hadn't been to see her since he'd come down from Oxford, and one day Beryl Tarkinton let drop casually that everyone knew Jerome was making a positive cake of himself dangling after Bella Langford. Sara kept her composure for the few minutes it took to get rid of her young swain and gain the privacy of her room to indulge in a hearty cry. When Jerome rode over to The Close a few days later to pay his respects to her parents and call on the little girl of his childhood, he brought a small box of bonbons for Mrs. Huntley and some hair ribbons for Sara who refused to come down to greet him. Angry and somehow hurt, he thrust the small packet at Mrs. Huntley.

"Some ribbons for Sara," he mumbled. Mrs. Huntley merely thanked him, but her husband, concerned over Sara's wan looks of the past week, discerned the reason and decided to tip the word to Jerome.

"Tell me," Mr. Huntley asked, "how long has it been since you've seen Sara?"

The young man wrinkled his brow. "Christmas holiday? No, I think perhaps it was even before that!"

"Then perhaps I should tell you that Sara's other gentlemen callers usually bring posies or something of the kind."

"Gentlemen callers!" Jerome snorted, then recalled himself. "Begging your pardon, sir, but I cannot imagine little Sara with 'gentlemen callers'! Why she is not yet sixteen!"

Mr. Huntley smiled to himself realizing Jerome was in for quite a shock when he saw Sara for the first time in so many months.

A few days later Sara was throwing bread to the ducks on the little pond and was bitterly castigating Jerome in her mind. Coming through the woods, he'd seen her sitting there with her back to him. Silently he crept up and put his hands over her eyes. She recognized his laugh and tried to pull his hands away from her face.

"Go away! I hate you!" she cried, "You are too fine for your old friends now. Go and dance attendance on Bella Langford like a tame monkey. Only leave me alone!"

"Are you crying, Sara?" Jerome asked incredulously.

"Do you think I'd cry over you, you great gawk!" she responded, breaking free and rolling over on the grass with her face buried in her arms. Jerome watched for a few seconds as her shoulders shook with sobs.

"Then who is making you cry? Tell me at once, Sara!" he commanded. He was bewildered and angered by an unaccountable stab of jealousy, for Sara was acting exactly like his cousin Letty did when she was in a miff over some boy.

"Tell me who it is and I'll break his head!" he ordered ferociously. He knelt down and took Sara by the shoulders, turning her on her side.

Sara, having a lively sense of the ridiculous which Jerome never shared, took one look at his fierce face and collapsed flat on her back in a fit of giggles, the tears still damp on her cheeks.

Jerome, indignant at this turn of events, almost boxed her ears. Instead he took her again by the shoulders and shook her.

"You stupid girl!" he exclaimed.

"*You* are the stupid one!" Sara said, sobering. "And I am not a girl any longer. If you had the sense to see the end of your nose you would realize it."

Finally Jerome *did* see. And what he saw was a marvelous revelation. Somehow in the few months he had been away, the little girl who had been his companion in his childhood years had blossomed startlingly. The thin arms he had likened to "pipestems" were amazingly transformed into unmistakably feminine limbs, and the former flat little girl's chest showed a soft swelling of rounded bosom beneath the taut muslin bodice.

He paused, his hands still on her dimpled shoulders, and searched her face, trying to find the hero-worshiping friend of his youth. Instead he found himself looking into the blue-gray eyes of a lovely and desirable young woman, a woman who made him feel, strangely, as no other woman ever had. Jerome wanted to lower himself on to that soft tempting body, kiss her trembling mouth, explore the beautiful and mysterious changes that had occurred in his Sara. With an oath, he flung himself away from her.

She sat up and smoothed her hair which had escaped in silken strands from under her embroidered headband. She was afraid she had angered him.

"Jerome?" she questioned hesitantly. When he didn't answer, she rose to her feet and went to him, taking his arm in hers as she had used to do when he was in the sulks. Jerome pulled away, not meeting her eyes.

"Oh, Jerome! Let's not quarrel. I'm sorry I laughed, but I wasn't laughing at you, truly I wasn't!" She started to fling her arms around his neck as she had done so many times in the past when childish anger had flared between them. His arms shot up to grasp her hands and push them away, but as their eyes met they both stopped, frozen in time for a long moment.

Sara's breath caught. He slid his hands down her arms, caressing her smooth contours. Then he took her shoulders and pulled her against his chest in the slow purposeful movements of someone in a dream. Sara tilted her face up to receive his kiss—her first kiss—and from the man she loved. His kiss was long and gentle, tasting her lips, while his hands smoothed over and over the muslin fabric that covered her back, awakening exciting and frightening emotions in her.

When he released her, Sara's knees almost buckled beneath her. They didn't speak. Jerome held out his hand in silence and she put her little hand into it, and as if by mutual consent they turned and headed behind the shrubbery, and down the little path that led to the home wood. There Jerome again took her in his arms and they kissed.

"Oh, Sara," he breathed at last into her hair. "Oh, Sara!" he could say nothing else.

"I love you, Jerome," Sara said simply, tracing a line with her fingers across his cheek and down to his jawline.

They kissed and lay down side by side with their arms around each other, content with the closeness of the moment. Then they kissed once more and the sudden flare of passion that burst upon them frightened them both with its intensity. They stood up, quickly.

"Sara, we cannot do this again!" Jerome said shakily.

"Why not?" Sara gave a little cry of dismay.

"Sara, Sara! You are too young to understand what can happen with a man and woman. I must protect your innocence, protect you from my baser nature until such a time as we can be married."

"Then you do love me!" Sara whispered, her voice filled with joy and triumph. She wanted to tell him she was not too young, that she did understand and if they loved each other everything would be all right; she wanted to throw herself upon him, to have him take her and set the seal of their love. Something made her hold back. Not fear, nor even a sense of propriety although her response to Jerome's violent lovemaking had shocked the gently-bred girl.

"What shall we do?" she asked when she regained a measure of control.

"I shall tell your father we love each other and ask him to give me your hand when you are seventeen on your next birthday," Jerome stated, solemnly.

"But that is almost a year away!" Sara stamped her feet in frustration, becoming for a moment the little girl he used to know so well. She tried to take his arm but he pulled away.

"I vow on this day that I will have no other woman to wife. I will not dishonor you with my coarse ways again!" he said, and Sara recognized his voice and stance as that of Sir Lancelot when they had played at being characters from King Arthur's Round Table. "I will not touch you again till then!"

"Oh, bother your vows!" she said angrily and turning on her heel ran back toward the house looking more like a wild gipsy girl with her skirts hiked up over her ankles than a would-be Guinevere.

Of course her parents refused to allow a courtship until she made her come-out and had at least one Season. They wanted her to get a taste of the larger world before casting her lot with the young man she'd loved since childhood. But just before her seventeenth birthday, her parents' dreams for her came to an end. They were killed when their carriage was overturned on a peaceful winding country road by a drunken young dandy trying to cut a figure as a whip.

The house was silent and dim with the shutters drawn; the great door knocker and all the mirrors were covered with crepe. It was a time of strangers who were her parents' relatives sitting in the places where she was accustomed to see her pretty mother or gallant father. It was a time of interminable days and infinite nights when she would weep into her pillow until the feathers were matted together. It was a time of whispering and sidelong glances from the neighbors and some of the relatives that filled her with dread despite the sympathy that was evident. The safe, loving world of Sara's girlhood crumbled around her and on the day of the double funeral, the final blow came.

She was standing outside near the library windows. "Do you mean to say the child has not been told yet?" she heard a voice question. "Why, that is monstrous! You must give her some time to adjust to the idea...and ...and, for heaven's sake, merely to pick up her trinkets and mementoes!"

"Now, Augusta," a man said—and Sara recognized the voice of her flabby middle-aged cousin Alfred—"the more time the chit has to think about leaving The Close, the harder it will be on her. And it's not as if she won't be coming back here someday, for she will return here when the mourning period is over as my bride!" His voice was smug.

"Well, I'm going to talk to Sir Robert right now and protest this unseemly haste!" the woman replied.

"Don't meddle, Augusta!" Alfred answered.

"You may have inherited an entailed estate, Alfred, but you are not the girl's guardian, Sir Robert is!" the woman's voice said, quivering with distaste.

"Well," the man said in a heated tone, "do your best, but Sir Robert is of the same mind. Sara will stay with them at Briarly for the year of mourning. Then after a very brief courtship," his voice continued with a sneer, "I will bring my little bride back to her home. Everybody will be happy. The girl in the home of her childhood— and I'm sure she will be heartily homesick after a year at Briarly—and me with a dainty little wife to break in. Sir Robert will be quit of a trust he don't fancy in the least nor does his wife. She don't take kindly to having a Swan in her chicken yard!"

"Then you are two of a kind, and I am heartily disgusted with you both. Why every feeling must be offended! That

sweet child, carried away from her home without a fare-
thee-well and, I have no doubt, *badgered* into marriage
with a hardened profligate like yourself!" The woman
stood up and Sara was able to see enough to recognize
her. It was Augusta Roche, Jerome's aunt by marriage,
and a childhood friend of her late mother.

What else transpired in the library, Sara never knew,
for once the initial shock left her, she ran into the woods
like a wild thing, racing through brambles and thickets
until her black dress and black lisle stockings were torn
in a hundred places. When it was noticed she was missing,
it was at first thought that she had gone off somewhere
and cried herself to sleep.

Gussie, returned to her sister-in-law's home, had the
story of Sara's fate out. No one realized when Jerome
slipped out of the room and it was past dinner time before
his absence was noted. "Oh," his Aunt Elston said, "he
is probably out mooning over Sara's departure; the silly
lad has fancied himself in love with her for several months.
Well, Alfred Huntley is not the man I'd have chosen for
such a young girl, but perhaps he will settle down after
marriage."

Gussie remained silent. She knew too well the rumors
that Alfred was involved with the scandalous Hell Club
and could only hope he was not so depraved as to initiate
an innocent young girl in its habits.

When evening came and Jerome had not returned home,
Gussie hoped he had done as he once threatened. He'd
told Gussie that when Sara turned seventeen if her parents
didn't give consent, he would carry her over the border
to Gretna Green and marry her out of hand. At the time
Gussie had only smiled and shaken her head, for Jerome
spent so much time with his nose in a book and his head
in the clouds that it was a rare day when his idealism was
translated into action. Still, when his sense of chivalry was

roused, he could be obsessed until his mission was accomplished.

Gussie was right in her suspicions, for when Jerome flew from the house he headed for just one place. There was a little copse in the woods near a winding stream where bluebells grew in the spring, but the place was so bounded by brambles and thorns that no one visited it except the wild creatures—and Sara and Jerome. When they were children it was Queen Guinevere's bower, or Morgan le Fay's secret tower or any one of a myriad make-believe places. As they grew older, the copse was a quiet and tranquil place to read or dream, and they had vowed once, that if either of them were in dire trouble, they would meet there.

For just one fleeting second Jerome doubted, for since the discovery of their love for each other, they had not visited this special place together, knowing perhaps where the beauty and isolation of the woods might lead them. Then he spotted Sara sitting in the dappled light, leaning against a clump of birches. She sat so still and straight that she frightened him, and Jerome pushed his way through the brambles, heedless of the scratches of the thorns.

"Sara!" he called softly. "Sara!"

When she didn't turn he broke through the last of the brush and ran to her. Her face was as white as the flowers that grew in little clusters near her feet, and her blue-gray eyes seemed darker. He stopped as he saw the torn sleeve and bodice of her black mourning dress, the dark bruises on her soft shoulder.

He threw himself to his knees. "What has happened?" he cried, fearing before she finally spoke just what her words must be.

"I'll kill him!" he raged.

"No. No . . ." Sara said. "He didn't . . . do anything

. . . I ran away when I overheard his plans, but I stumbled and fell and tore my clothes on brambles."

"We'll go where he can't hurt you," Jerome promised, soothing her, gently rubbing her shoulder where thorns had ripped her dress. He kissed the soft flesh where the bruises showed, then kissed her cheeks where the tears streamed down silently.

"Oh, Jerome," Sara said tremblingly, returning his kiss. She felt his hand smoothing her shoulder, slipping inside her bodice to cup her breast and she wondered that it felt so right, so natural to feel his touch where no hand had caressed before. She arched her back, offering herself to his warm, seeking mouth, unprepared for the spasm of desire that coursed through them both. Gently, he lowered her to the mossy ground. And there in the copse where two children had become friends, the two friends became lovers.

Afterward, Sara changed into one of his cousin's dresses that Jerome had brought in a duffel along with some bread and cheese, and within an hour they were on a stage headed toward Scotland.

There followed a trying time for the young lovers as a result of their elopement and the scandal that was whispered.

"Ah, Jerome," Sara now sighed aloud. "What children we were then!" Usually she avoided thinking of the past, especially of her intimate life with Jerome. It was so dreadfully disturbing. But it was Augusta who'd inspired this flight into memory, Gussie who'd taken the young couple in and given out that they had been betrothed that summer, Gussie who'd managed to shame Sir Robert into signing an agreement for Sara's dowry. She had provided a home for Sara and Jerome, sharing her limited resources with love and generosity.

CHAPTER FOUR

Sara went in search of her aunt, but Gussie was nowhere to be found. At last a small sound from above-stairs sent her up to the attics where she found Augusta happily rummaging through boxes and trunks like a child opening Christmas packages.

"Only look, Sara! I have found all the lovely silks and shantungs I bought before...before we moved into this house," she caught herself. "This puce satin too!"

Sara stared, for Gussie's eyes were shining and even the smudge on her nose didn't detract from her comely looks. Gussie pulled out a length of Brussels lace from one trunk and draped it aournd her shoulders with a flourish.

"No, I haven't lost my senses, Sara. It's just that these lovely fabrics and laces almost make me feel young again."

"Oh, Aunt! You are still young and look charmingly!" Tears started in Sara's eyes and she bit her lip in dismay. "I have only just now realized how selfish I've become, keeping you sequestered here with me. I am so truly sorry."

"Hush, hush!" Gussie swept Sara into her arms. "I have loved living quietly here. You must not say such things. Indeed, I was burnt to the socket and needed a bit of retirement."

Sara knew the good-natured, reassuring lie for what it was, but there seemed little more to say for the moment. It wasn't until one morning a few days later when they were sipping coffee and reading the morning post that Sara had the chance—at last—to set things right. As she separated the bills and announcements into neat piles, she was regaled by her aunt's disjointed comments on her social correspondence.

"...Oh! Euphronia Attlesly has finally managed to foist her eldest daughter onto some baronet...five thousand a year...poor man! What a pack of ne'er-do-well relatives he'll inherit . . . Well, I imagine he is no bargain . . . iron legs...how droll!"

"Oh, no, Aunt! You cannot hoax me. Even Mrs. Attlesly would not be so cruel as to marry her daughter to a man with an iron leg!" Sara teased.

"No, you terrible creature! Maria is to wed Sir Bartholomew Hatcher and you well know he does not have an iron leg. The legs are on a *couch* Euphronia has purchased," Gussie replied in mock dudgeon. "Really Sara, how can I possibly read any sense into my mail when you are constantly diverting me with your remarks."

"*I*, diverting *you?*" Sara laughed as she refilled their cups.

They ate in companionable silence for a few moments.

Gussie opened a cream-colored envelope and scanned the crossed and recrossed lines. Her brow puckered.

"Sara," she exclaimed. "You will never guess what has happened."

"Why, of course I can," Sara replied. "You have been asked to lead a crusade to the Holy Land. No, let me think," she continued as her aunt smiled indulgently. "You have received a proposal of marriage from the Regent and leave immediately to set up housekeeping!"

"Tiresome child! I have received a letter from my dear cousin Amelia Bensome. She has been in indifferent health for some years but was hoping to give her only daughter, Amanda, a come-out this Season; now the doctor informs her she can on no account leave the quiet of Hampshire for the rigors of London. So..." Gussie stuttered to a halt.

The gleam in her aunt's eyes revealed all to Sara and happily, though not without some trepidation, she seized the opportunity to make amends.

"But *you* must sponsor Amelia's daughter, dearest Gussie! Nothing less will do!"

"Do you mean it?"

"How could I not?"

"Oh! You are the most precious creature! The best of friends!" Gussie beamed, already peeling off the layers of shawls and other props from the swiftly forgotten invalid pose. "I will write Amelia straight away! If the daughter has one tenth the beauty of the mother, we shall set all of London on its ear. And," she continued, "it is about time that you reentered Society. You are much too young to bury yourself here."

Sara gasped in dismay. "Do not include me in your schemes. It must be understood from the start that while I will welcome Miss Bensome to our home, you cannot expect me to attend any of the teas or balls or routs, for indeed I will not!"

"Whatever you wish, child, although I think it would do you a world of good to get out and enjoy yourself. But I will say no more on that subject." And with a surprising lightness of foot, Gussie was off to write her note and set things in motion.

She smiled at her aunt's happiness but was adamant that she would not let them involve her in the social whirl. No, Sara thought. There was no need for her aunt to include her in all the plans. She was much too busy. And the parties were composed of gimlet-eyed mamas and schoolgirl misses and condescending peeresses . . . and handsome rakes, perhaps even that provoking gentleman with the golden lights in his dark eyes

Augusta was in high spirits. The little bottles of vinaigrette and hartshorn in their pretty frosted vials disappeared from the solar, the bedchamber and the sitting room.

"My dear," she burst out the next afternoon, "we simply *must* procure some new clothing! I've been through my entire wardrobe and there is not *one* walking dress or gown or *anything* which is not so sadly out of style as to be positively *dowdy!*"

This won a peal of laughter from Sara, for if there was one thing Gussie was not, it was a dowd! Her small jointure was handsomely supplemented by funds Sara provided, and even though the two women lived a very quiet social life, Gussie was always rigged out in the latest fashions. Indeed, only the previous week she had received delivery on two morning dresses and one tea gown from Madame Francot.

"It is no laughing matter," Gussie chided, although there was a corresponding laugh in her eyes. "I will not be seen at Almack's or any of the *ton* parties looking like some shabby-genteel relation and embarrass Amelia's daughter. Why it could be fatal to our attempt to fire her off well!"

"*Our* attempt, Aunt?" Sara exclaimed, somewhat taken aback. "My part in this campaign is merely to provide support for young Miss Bensome's assault on society; *you* are the general."

"Don't think of this as a battle, I pray you! I conceive it as the unveiling of a new masterpiece, the launching of a new ship . . ." She waved her arms dramatically. "It will be such a lark to send Amelia's daughter off in proper style! Why we made our own bows into Polite Society together. And if not a woman of superior understanding, Amelia is of good heart with very winning ways, and a face, I daresay, which would still cause many a second glance." She moved restlessly but gracefully around the room with her usual vitality and flair.

"I must admit," Sara said, "it *will* be rather interesting. Especially if the girl should be dumpy or hatchet-faced; I will like to see what you may make of her!"

"Terrible child!" Gussie denounced Sara. "If you only knew Amelia Bensome you would *know* that she could never be so declassé as to have a frumpy child." Gussie's severe accents were belied by her dancing eyes. "And speaking of 'frumpy,' if I may be so bold . . ." Her brows were raised high as she stared meaningly at Sara's black bombazine morning dress.

"Do you feel I will detract from your consequence if anyone spies me in such an outmoded garment?" Sara's mouth twitched with amusement. "Well, perhaps you are right. I will tell Witherall to hire us a carriage for one o'clock and we will shop, if not to your heart's content, at least not to the detriment of my sure-to-be aching feet."

"We shall have a marvelous afternoon!" Gussie prophesied. And, after their first stop at Madame Franchot's, Sara was inclined to agree, even though she knew she disappointed the modiste by refusing to consider a gown of amber crepe or a walking dress of cerise silk trimmed with black cording. At least she did not reduce that lady to a state of spasm by refusing to heed Gussie's pleas to discard her dark grays and blacks in favor of becoming blues and mauves.

"We cannot have you going about like a black crow any longer!" Augusta declared adamantly. "If we are to take our proper places in Society we must do it up right and tight."

"Dear Gussie," Sara had to remind her more than once, "do not think you will drag me to *all* the *ton* parties, for there I draw the line. However," she relented, "a few drives and perhaps some little suppers or theater parties from our home . . . but never, *never* will you convince me to attend Almack's or any of those other fashionable squeezes. You and Miss Bensome may gallivant all over town with my blessing if you don't include me in all your plans!

Augusta desisted then and turned back to the matter of Sara's clothing.

With her love of textures and colors, Sara was much easier to persuade than Gussie anticipated, though the fabrics she chose were more subdued than her aunt would have liked. A visit to Madame Celeste and Madame Solange further rounded out the new wardrobes for the two ladies, leaving only a visit to the Pantheon Bazaar to purchase silk stockings and trimmings.

They returned home laden with parcels and packages. Sara went up to her room to deposit some of the smaller bundles and left the rest for Witherall to fetch up the rather steep stairs. She took off her walking dress and began to hang it up carefully, suddenly eyeing it with dislike.

"Horrors!" she exclaimed, depositing the dress in a heap on the floor.

Nothing hanging in the armoire pleased her, so she opened one of the boxes from Solange's establishment and removed a gown of navy blue silk with pale gray grosgrain ribbons at the cuffs and down the bodice. She had to wear it, for she had developed a sudden overwhelming distaste for anything more somber. Taking the plunge, she finished her toilette quickly and descended the stairs to the drawing room.

If Sara had expected to surprise Gussie with her new look, she was doomed to disappointment. Her aunt stood by the fireplace, assessing the room with an apparently jaundiced eye. Gussie waited, however, until they were both fortified by quantities of hot tea with milk, sponge cake and cinnamon tartlets before edging toward the topic foremost in her mind.

"Sara, dear, I think perhaps a little tea party very soon? Quite small and quite select to create our first ripple in the social stream."

"That sounds lovely. Let us invite my cousin Maria, Lady Linville and Miss Linville by all means. And I will leave the rest of the guest list to your capable hands."

"Oh, indeed we *must* invite Maria Sefton. If she approves of Miss Bensome's style, she will no doubt obtain vouchers for Almack's for us. Lavinia Linville and her daughter will open many doors for our protégé, too. There isn't a mean bone in either of their bodies, and besides Miss Linville is almost engaged to Lord Oakley." Gussie clapped her hands. "I'm sure we can send Amelia's daughter off very creditably indeed!"

"I'm beginning to dread the sound of the word 'we,'" Sara laughed, refilling their teacups.

Augusta sipped her tea and resumed her measuring looks about the room, interspersed with an occasional significant glance at Sara, who was doing her best to supress her rising mirth.

"What is it, Augusta? You are making the most extraordinary faces!"

"It is those hideous chairs by the bow window! I cannot conceive how we have been able to sit day after day in the same room with such ill-designed pieces of furniture! And the upholstery is positively...Medieval!" Gussie said.

"But it was *supposed* to make them look Medieval," Sara burst out in a chuckle, "for they were originally in the solar, you know."

"Yes, well. That is nothing to the fact they are simply frightful. I think I will purchase some new ones, along with a little sofa and a *tête-à-tête* in the newer style," she went on speaking almost to herself, "perhaps in the classical mode."

Sara looked about the room. In truth it *was* getting a bit shabby. And if they refurnished, they would also have to refurbish, for new curtains and draperies would be musts.

"And definitely a new carpet!" Gussie said aloud, almost as if reading Sara's mind.

"Well," Sara said, resigned, "if we are going to decorate afresh we might as well do it all at once and get it over with and not piecemeal. What do you think, Aunt? Can it be done in time?"

"Just leave it all in my hands, my child," Gussie announced. "I will handle all the arrangements and you will have nothing to do but sit back and be amazed!"

"Good Lord! You aren't planning on Egyptian Pharaoh furniture . . . or . . . or, Heaven forbid . . . iron legs!" Sara said, unable to hide her laughter.

"Oh, tush! You know my taste better than that! I would like you to come along with me a morning or two so we can put our heads together and decide just what might suit."

Sara agreed to this, and if her thoughts were a bit rueful, she couldn't help but acknowledge to herself that she found Gussie's excitement contagious. Her nature was such that while she disciplined herself for her painting, she still retained a tremendous amount of energy and passion for any new project which caught her fancy. Once her mind was set on a certain path she followed it wholeheartedly. Therefore, it was with an interest almost as great as her aunt's that she set out with that lady the next day to begin the selection of new drawing-room furniture.

Once in the various shops and establishments Sara and Augusta found it impossible to stop with rosewood furniture and a Chinese rug in blue, gold and white for the drawing room. In fact, their recollections of the little sitting room and the cozy dining room at their house on Green Dolphin Street were quite lowering in view of the new furnishings for the drawing room. By mutual agreement the two ladies decided to throw caution to the winds and include the aforementioned rooms. When the fabrics for the draperies and undercurtains had been decided upon, Gussie suggested they walk part of the way home to clear away the cobwebs after being cooped up in musty rooms all day. While Sara smiled to think how the proprietor would pale to hear his immaculately elegant and airy show-rooms being called "musty," she couldn't help but agree that some fresh air would be welcome.

Strolling down the street, Gussie encountered several of her friends who expressed delight that she and Sara would be enlivening what might turn out otherwise to be a rather flat season. As they continued on their way Sara recognized the spare muscular figure of "the gentleman from America" descending from a smart black barouche. He assisted a lady in alighting from the vehicle, and then,

as he turned back to say a word to the groom, he spotted
Sara and her companion. With a flash of white teeth in
his tanned face, he swept them a most distinguished bow.
Sara returned his greeting with a nod and a smile. As soon
as they were out of sight Gussie turned to her accusingly.

"I did not know you numbered such an interesting man
among your acquaintance," she questioned with an arch
smile. "Indeed, I thought I knew all the gentlemen who
had been introduced to you. Pray, who is that striking
fellow?"

"Well, that I do not know *exactly*, so don't badger me
for an introduction!" Sara replied in the same measure.
"He is the fond father of a young lady and has just commissioned me to do her portrait. All I know of him is that
he is an American who is somehow involved in shipping.
Oh, yes," she added, "and a widower."

"Is he, now?"

"Don't go matchmaking, Aunt, or I declare I'll lock
myself in the studio and leave you high and dry with Miss
Bensome!"

"I know you could not do such a shabby thing, child,"
Gussie replied. She said no more on that head, but continued to eye Sara from time to time with a certain look
which communicated all too well her intent to embark on
yet another new venture.

Since the day was so fine they decided to stroll all the
way home. Rounding the corner into Upper Turney Place
a sleek racing curricle in walnut and yellow bowled by at
a spanking pace. The driver, finely turned out in a many-
caped coat of buff and a tall beaver hat, saluted Sara with
a slight smile as he swept on down the street without
checking his speed.

"Coo! He din' 'arf shave t' buldin'!" a grimy street
urchin shouted to his companion. "Bangers!" he continued
as he raced away. This remark, while fairly unintelligible

to Sara and Gussie, still left them without a doubt that it was a tribute to the driver's skill.

"And who was that?" Gussie inquired. "Are you also commissioned to do *his* daughter's portrait? If so, I may be inclined to take up painting myself!"

Sara flushed a bit. "No, I am doing a portrait of the gentleman himself."

After tea the two ladies parted, Sara to work in her studio, and Gussie to send out cards announcing the emergence once more of the Mesdames Roche into the fashionable whirl of the *beau monde*.

CHAPTER FIVE

Even before the arrival of Miss Bensome in Green Dolphin Street, a steady flow of calling cards had been left with the delighted Witherall. The daily post increased until a veritable torrent of engagement cards and invitations were littered in haphazard piles on Augusta's secretaire.

"Listen, my dear," she asked Sara one day, "do you think you and Miss Bensome would rather attend a balloon ascension on the eighteenth or a tea at Lady Hendricke's town house?"

"The balloon ascension by all means. I know few girls of seventeen who would forego such a spectacle for a tea-with-the-tabbies! To be honest, I would enjoy it more, too. What is the sense of finally getting out of this house only to have tea in another?"

Gussie had to admit the logic of this statement. She

nibbled on the end of her pen gently as she sorted through more of the cards. "Would you consider attending the Favershams' ball on the twenty-second?" she ventured.

"Not unless I lose my wits between now and then," Sara said adamantly. "I will see a few of our acquaintances and attend the lesser festivities, but nothing will persuade me to parade like a performing monkey before all those tattle-mongers who wagged their tongues and shook their heads when Jerome died!"

Seeing that she would not change her mind, Gussie let the matter rest. "One last thing, Sara," she continued. "Lady St. Martin is planning a picnic soon if the weather holds. Do you think Miss Bensome would like to attend, since Lady St. Martin has kindly invited her also."

"Why don't you ask her yourself?" Sara answered, seeing a hackney pull up at the curb. "If that is not she descending from that carriage, I will be much surprised."

Indeed, Gussie exclaimed, the dainty girl alighting with her abigail in tow was very like her parent.

Gussie threw down her pen, straightened her coiffure and flew out into the entrance hall to greet her guest. The rest of the afternoon was spent in getting acquainted and hearing all the latest news from Hampshire. The two ladies of Green Dolphin Street acknowledged Miss Bensome was all they had hoped: as sweet as she was pretty. Although quite shy, her charming ways and good nature were such, they thought, as were bound to please the most severe critic.

Before a day had passed, the two younger women were on a first-name basis and Gussie had become "Aunt" to Amanda Bensome. And in the days that followed Gussie and Amanda were more frequently out than in and receiving guests. Fortunately then for Sara, it was not often that she was obliged to join them and play hostess. She was determined to exert herself on another matter, though.

She took Amanda in hand for shopping, since she did not quite trust that Gussie's flair for the dramatic would be overcome by common sense in dressing a young girl fresh from the schoolroom.

Two afternoons were spent in visiting various dressmakers and in purchasing silk stockings, and azure and daffodil kid gloves. Their last stop was at a milliner's shop on River Street noted for its charming confections. While Amanda debated over the merits of a chip straw hat with cherry ribbons versus a striking but more demure one with a sprig of forget-me-nots over one ear, Sara eyed the other attractions. Among the rainbow colored hats was one Sara thought might be suitable for herself—a blue satin turban trimmed with small bands of black velvet. She put it on and dubiously eyed her reflection in the mirror. Definitely dowdy, she thought and was surprised to hear her words echoed aloud! Over her shoulder in the mirror appeared the smiling countenance of the Earl of Ramsey, still known to Sara as "the gentleman who waited," and ever more often as "that man."

"I would suggest," he said, "the white one with the red cabbage roses."

"I wouldn't think of wearing such a hat!" Sara responded before she could stop herself.

"More's the pity," the Earl replied. "If you wish to be stared at it might as well be for being dashing as for being drab!"

Before she could answer he had turned on his heel and walked away. She watched in the mirror as he joined his companion, an exceptionally attractive woman with hair of an improbable red. The woman glanced at Sara disparagingly and made some laughing comment to the gentleman behind a suede-gloved hand. This so enraged Sara that she bought two rather daring hats: one was french blue with white swansdown trimming; the other was a glowing russet with an impertinent feather curving down along her cheek. Since the hackney was stacked with parcels and packages, the milliner promised to deliver the ladies' purchases to their doorstep that afternoon.

Tea was served shortly after their arrival back at Green Dolphin Street and as bandboxes arrived from the milliner's during, tea, it was not until much later that Sara retired to inspect her purchases. When she found three hatboxes in her room she thought Witherall had carried up one of Amanda's purchases by mistake.

She opened one box and removed the russet hat. The second box, however, contained not the French-blue chapeau nor one of Amanda's selections, but the frilly white hat with the extravagant cabbage roses. Tucked into one of the roses was a plain card inscribed in a bold masculine hand, "with my compliments on your come-out." Even in her anger Sara felt a flash of appreciation for such audacity before righteous indignation won. She thought of cutting the hat into pieces, but better sense prevailed. Then she thought of the very thing. She would present the hat to her aunt, who with her junoesque frame and dramatic air could carry off even the most daring of styles.

"That man," Sara fumed. She was incensed he would put her in the same category with the bit-of-muslin he had accompanied to the milliner's shop. Her life, so orderly and peaceful such a short time before, was drifting out of her control. She paced, thinking furiously. Very well! She would finish the portrait of that maddening gentleman as soon as possible and then put him firmly out of her mind. Once the portrait was finished, there would be no need ever to see him again. Sara refused to investigate the bleakness that this last thought conjured up, and went in search of Gussie, carrying the hatbox out in front of her as if she were afraid it might bite! Yet somehow it never entered her head to cancel his appointment.

The Earl, meanwhile, found himself strangely reluctant to bring up the subject of setting a date for his marriage. In fact he was relieved that Pamela's mother refused to have an announcement of the engagement placed in the *Gazette* as yet.

At the next sittings Sara was determined to ignore her attraction to the Earl and was as businesslike and curt as possible. His handsome face set, his manner cool and forbidding, the Earl was equally grim. Finally the stern set of his countenance unnerved Sara during one sitting.

"Don't glare at me so!" she ordered imperiously. "It is not at all the look I wish to capture."

"I am not glaring!" the Earl said icily, his forehead creasing even more severely.

"Take a turn around the room and relax. You are positively frightening me!"

"I would like to meet any man who could frighten you!" he replied as he approached the easel.

Disconcerted, Sara took a step backward, her dark-fringed eyes widening in alarm. Instantly his face softened.

"Forgive me, ma'am. I thought you were in jest. I had no idea I was so fearsome."

"No, no!" Sara flushed. "I . . . I was just startled for a moment . . . I was lost in concentration . . ." She trailed off in confusion, flushing.

"Was it the hat?" he asked contritely. "Indeed, I meant no offense. My friends have *told* me that my impulsiveness would be my downfall. I didn't stop to think that a Lady of Quality would interpret my behavior as an insult. I do beg your pardon, ma'am!" He smiled down at her.

Sara continued to look at the floor as a rosy blush spread over her cheeks. The Earl hesitated a second, then with one finger lifted her chin until he could look full into her face.

"Come, forgive me," he said softly. "You must admit it is a very fetching hat!"

Sara smiled tremulously, undone by his warmth. The responsive glow of his eyes made her catch her breath. He put his hands on her shoulders to draw her closer. She didn't resist, swept along by the moment.

Suddenly there was a terrible din in the entryway and the door to the studio flew open to show a distracted Witherall, wig askew and dressed in a groom's livery. With no preamble he burst out: "Lor', miss! Your h'ant's fall'n down t' stars!"

Sara and the Earl rushed out to find a much-shaken Augusta lying in the hallway at the foot of the stairs, her face pale except for the dark bruise already rising along her hairline. Sara stepped forward to comfort her aunt while the Earl deftly probed Gussie's swollen ankle for broken bones.

"A bad sprain, nothing cracked that I can tell," he announced. Turning to Witherall he said, ". . . er. . . . Wither*ly?* . . . I assume?"

"Wither*bee!*" the butler in groom's guise responded hotly.

"Fetch the doctor at once. I will carry your mistress up to her room, and Madame Roche will make her as comfortable as possible until your return."

As Witherall exited he almost collided with the tall American gentleman who was just about to rap on the door. For once Edward was glad to see him, and the two men carried Gussie up to her boudoir. The conglomeration of roses and ruffles and pillows struck the Earl quite speechless. But the American with his refreshing openness of speech declared it a delightful room and so like a rose bower as he had never seen anywhere.

Neither the American nor, apparently, the gratified Gussie noted any impropriety in a gentleman comparing, however favorably, one lady's boudoir to others he had seen. It was left to Sara and the Earl, then, to stifle their mirth as best they could. Their eyes met and brimmed over with laughter.

Sara rang the bell for the parlor maid futilely, remembering at last that it was the maid's afternoon off. Since she could not leave her aunt, the surprising American retired to the depths of the kitchen to prepare some tea, and the Earl went downstairs to kick his heels and await the doctor.

In a short time Witherall and the doctor arrived and went upstairs; half an hour passed and the Earl was seized with the realization that while he waited downstairs in the parlor, the American had not returned. The man was altogether too encroaching, he determined with annoyance. New World manners were one thing, but to remain where he was neither needed nor wanted! Angrily, he thought that perhaps the American's presence *was* wanted. Well, he had better things to do and would be on his way. He would send a note around in the morning with his compliments to the elder Madame Roche and wish her a swift recovery.

As the Earl rose to leave, the gentleman he had just been consigning to the devil in his thoughts came into the room with a ready grin.

"You were right, sir. Just some bruises and a very bad strain that will keep the lady in bed for a few days." He extended his hand. "Christopher Ames, of Albemarle County, Virginia, at your service, sir!"

Ramsey could not be so ungracious as to refuse the hand offered him. He bowed rather stiffly. "I am Ramsey," he said in cool accents.

"Pleased to make your acquaintance," Ames responded. "Well, I must be off, if I'm to return in time to escort them to Lady Linville's ball tonight. As Miss Gussie's laid up, I offered to take Miss Bensome in my carriage with my daughter and me." The gentlemen bowed and the American took his leave.

"Miss Gussie indeed!" the Earl muttered under his breath.

"Sir?" questioned Witherall who had just entered, once more dressed in his butler's attire.

"How is Madame Roche, Wither-What-Ever?" Edward asked scathingly.

"Madame is resting comfortably," the butler replied in his most disapproving accents. "Madame Sara Roche thanks you most kindly for your assistance and begs you not to put yourself out further. Madame will send a message round when she is ready to continue with the sittings." With this, he handed the Earl his hat and cane and ushered him out.

That evening the Earl was still in a state of indignation. While the American Mr. Ames was made free of the house on Green Dolphin Street and invited to call Augusta Roche by her Christian name—her pet name even—he, the Earl of Ramsey, had been dismissed like a schoolboy—and without a date set for the next session on his portrait!

He had to concede that his irritation was unreasonable. He had no claim on the ladies in Green Dolphin Street and therefore surely their friendships were none of his affair. And his betrothal, although as yet unofficial, still must exclude him from forming any interest in Sara Roche. These thoughts did nothing to soothe his temper and it was with some impatience that he made ready for Lady Linville's ball. The thought of again meeting Mr. Ames set his teeth on edge but he had promised his intended that he would put in an appearance and it was too late in the day to cry off. Besides, he admitted to himself, Sara might be there, and he was singularly interested in the provoking and lovely artist.

* * *

It was as crowded at the ball as Edward had foreseen which may have made for some discomfort to the guests, but proclaimed Lady Linville's party a great success by the *ton*. He had not seen his betrothed or her mother, and so joined the other men in the card room. He was found there by Binghampton who awarded him a heavy-handed pat on the shoulder and announced that he was "...a capital fellow and one to free all other men from being at the beck and call of the ladies"; for, he went on, "who but Ramsey would sit here calmly with his cronies while some damned American waltzed with his fiancée!"

The Earl left the card room abruptly only to have his worst fears confirmed. Lady Pamela, her neat blond head tilted coquettishly, was being whisked around the room by the inescapable Mr. Ames. As Edward stood there speechless, his eyes alighted on a familiar figure across the room. He gazed with admiration at Sara in a gown of heather-blue silk with a matching embroidered shawl draped loosely over her arms.

Sara looked up and met the Earl's gaze with surprise. In a trice Edward was across the floor and making a bow.

"You look charming! Will you waltz with me, ma'am?" Without waiting for a reply he took her hand to lead her into the dance. She demurred.

"I do not dance with gentlemen with whom I am un-acquainted."

"How can you say that after all the hours we have spent *alone* in each other's company?" the Earl replied with unnecessary volume.

Two formidable dowagers shot them a glance, and Sara realized there was no telling *what* the devilish man might say next. They moved out in the crowd, and she was gratified to find her partner was accomplished on the dance floor. As he swung her around to the strains of the waltz she was overly aware of his hand at her waist. Edward did not speak, but kept his eyes smiling down at her as if enchanted.

As for Sara, the exhilaration of being swept around a ballroom in the arms of a handsome man was a revelation. She didn't stop to question if it would be any man's arms that affected her so or if it were just something peculiar to this one man with the blazing topaz eyes.

When the music ended she quickly came back to earth as she was escorted to where Miss Bensome stood surrounded by a group of admirers. As he relinquished her hand, her partner bowed and smiled. "For future dances," he said in an undertone, "I am Edward, Lord Ramsey," and with a salute he was gone.

Mr. Ames, whose name had been made known to Sara after her aunt's unfortunate accident, came up to claim the next dance. Since it was a country dance, she did not have the opportunity to discover if dancing in Mr. Ames's arms would produce the same effect as dancing with the Earl; however she enjoyed the set thoroughly.

Mr. Ames solicited the honor of taking Sara into supper and they were joined by his daughter who was squired by an obviously smitten Lord Binghampton. Over small puffs filled with curried shrimp and veal tarts with cream sauce, Sara and Janie Ames renewed their acquaintance. Amanda sat nearby with Lord Trowbridge and another couple.

"Father," Janie inquired over a dessert of apricot trifle, "who is the lovely lady I saw you waltzing with just before supper? She is exquisite!"

"Lady Pamela, Lord Binghampton's sister," her parent replied with a bow to the young man. "Truly a most beautiful young woman!"

"Yes," Bing said with pride. "She's been the hit of the season. That is until you appeared on the scene, ma'am," he continued with a worshipful glance at Janie Ames.

"You took all the shine off her and I must say she don't like it a bit! Not that it makes any difference," he went on in some embarrassment, "for she's by way of being engaged but don't want it announced until we go to Ramsey Park after the season."

"Then it is Lord Ramsey she is affianced to!" Mr. Ames exclaimed. "Well, that's a surprise to me! Begging your pardon, but in my experience a knowing man of the world doesn't usually settle down with such a young miss."

In the stunned silence that followed no one noticed that Sara had paled visibly. Appalled at her father's remark, Janie smiled prettily and said "wasn't that the music starting up again?" and the party returned to the ballroom.

Mr. Ames apologized for embarrassing Sara with his forthrightness and she quickly put him at ease; she declined his invitation to the waltz that was just being struck up pleading a sudden headache. As the American escorted Sara to a quiet alcove, the Earl bore down on them.

"I believe this is my dance, Madame Roche," he intoned glibly.

"I have already promised this dance to Mr. Ames," Sara answered, and taking that astonished gentleman's arm, turned back to the dance floor. Mr. Ames, having had his home graced by a wife and a daughter, soon recovered himself and swept Sara out on to the polished parquet floor.

As they waltzed around the room, Sara found her falsehood about the headache had become quite true, and she attributed to this the fact that she did not enjoy her second waltz of the evening as much as the first. Not even the one glimpse she had of the Earl glowering on the sidelines had any hope of curing her ailment, and so pale and glassy-eyed was she as the dance ended that a concerned Mr. Ames declared he would escort her home immediately. In a short time Sara and a happy Amanda were home.

After checking on Augusta and finding her sleeping soundly, Sara bathed her temples in lavender water. Her heart bruised, Sara realized her folly in letting herself become interested again in a man; her original intent of keeping aloof from the world was a much less painful plan.

Only Augusta's mishap had gotten her out to attend the Linvilles' ball, and as soon as her aunt was recovered enough to chaperone their guest Sara could once more retreat to the safety of her very private life. At last, exhausted, she dropped into a fitful slumber. Once she dreamed that she was waltzing again with the Earl. She could feel his hand on her waist; when she awoke it was only Muse curled up into a small warm bundle at her back.

Early the next morning while most fashionable ladies were still asleep, Sara and Gussie were surprised to receive a visit from Mr. Christopher Ames and his daughter. They had called with a large pot of azaleas for the invalid. As Mr. Ames stated ingeniously, he could not expect to compete with Gussie's roses! The visitors had only meant to deliver the flowers along with their best wishes, but Gussie heard the voices and enjoined Sara to tell them they must come up and divert her at once before she succumbed to a fatal boredom. Since Mr. Ames would not allow of such a tragedy, the four spent a very merry morning ending with an invitation to the opera by Mr. Ames when Augusta should be on her feet again.

The Earl, meanwhile, had sent around a basket of plover eggs accompanied by a quail in aspic and a bottle of wine to strengthen the invalid and a brief note in his own hand. His morning was otherwise occupied by business and as he was engaged to take Lady Pamela on an excursion with several other young people, he had no time to inquire in person in Green Dolphin Street.

The Earl had bespoken luncheon at a comfortable inn

and as the party dined on country ham and mutton pie, the conversation drifted to the previous evening's events. After a few minutes the topic of interest focused on the American Mr. Ames and his lovely daughter.

"Rich as Croesus," one young buck was heard to say.

"Lord, yes!" Bing responded. "I've heard he's the warmest man in America. Why I vow he could buy and sell half of London with his pin money from the stories going round the clubs."

While Edward found that this news did little to endear Mr. Ames to himself, Lady Pamela displayed a rather excessive interest that only a questioning look from her betrothed prevented her from pursuing. Balked on this head, Pamela turned her tart tongue to the hapless daughter of Mr. Ames.

"Fie, Binghampton!" she chided her brother who was eulogizing the attributes of Janie Ames in flowing periods. "I do not see why you are in such transports over that girl. I grant you her features and manners are quite unexceptionable, but I cannot bring myself to believe that you admire such a tall and brown-skinned creature."

If Bing's defense of his goddess, which included such terms as "nymph" and "daughter of Diana" were not enough to deter Lady Pamela, the astounded looks on the faces of her admirers in the party were all that was needed to have her recall that such acidity did not suit her carefully nurtured pose of being all sugar and spice. Quickly Christopher and Janie Ames were dropped as a topic of discussion and Lady Pamela spent the ride back to town in exercising all her charms.

That evening the Earl joined his fiancée for what he thought was to be an intimate family dinner before an evening of opera. It was with mingled awe and resignation that he saw Mr. Ames and his daughter alighting from a carriage in St. James street before the very house where he had expected to dine *en famille*. Edward bowed to his nemesis and also to Miss Ames who was in exceptionally good looks in a dress of primrose muslin cut *à la Grec*.

"My," Mr. Ames hailed the Earl, "London Society must travel in small circles these days, for we are forever running into each other wherever we go!"

"Yes," sighed Edward, "and getting smaller all the time." They were ushered inside before the American could reply to this cryptic remark.

During dinner the Earl was placed beside Miss Ames on his hostess's right and found her to be as refreshingly natural as her parent. When he asked how she liked the gay round of balls and parties, he was startled by her answer.

"London is quite elegant and the people we have met have been very kind and hospitable," Janie Ames replied, "but it is difficult to tell who is friendly and who is just naturally kind, from those who are influenced by father's wealth."

The Earl gazed at her with a quizzical smile. "Surely at your age you should not be thinking such leveling thoughts," he stated. "You should be overcome and spend all your time planning on who shall fill your dance card or escort you to the latest pantomime rather than philosophizing on the sins of Society!"

Miss Ames smiled back at this and answered that pound dealing was her long suit. She had never been able to come up with artless responses but always spoke her mind before she could put a guard on her unruly tongue.

Ramsey remarked that he preferred straightforward answers and admired anyone who spoke with honesty rather than dealing in commonplaces. The two talked amiably during the first course and then turned to their other dinner partners with the next remove. Throughout the dinner whenever he faced down the long elegantly appointed table he was able to maintain conversation with Miss Ames and watch his fiancée in animated flirtation with Christopher Ames. Not even Lady Kennerly's keen eye was able to distract Pamela from her attempt to attach the American.

When the gentlemen remained behind over their port, Pamela's mother drew her aside on the pretext of a torn flounce, and led her into the small yellow saloon for a quick-to-the-point lecture.

". . . and I would have much more to say to you, young lady, but we must not absent ourselves from the drawing room for more than a few minutes. Take care that you do not cause Ramsey to suffer a revulsion of feelings toward you for he is mighty high in the instep and your shocking behavior must cause him embarrassment!"

"Fie, Mama!" her daughter responded too pertly. "Ramsey is too much the gentleman to cry off; and even if he takes me in disgust, there are more eligible gentlemen than he who would be honored if my choice were to fall on them!"

Lady Kennerly's hand itched to slap her daughter across her saucy cheek, and if there were not guests awaiting them she doubted that she would have shown forbearance. "If you mean Mr. Ames, what must he think of your coming behavior? He is perhaps not quite up to snuff for the highest circles, but even in America it must not be at all the thing for an affianced woman to flirt like a Coventry Garden miss in the presence of her betrothed!"

Pamela flounced out of the room and the seething Lady Kennerly had no recourse but to follow her. For the balance of the evening the young lady of the house divided herself equally among the guests, but whether this was due to her mother's admonitions or the fact that Mr. Ames would not be drawn into any *tête-à-têtes* was inconclusive. She did, however, manipulate an invitation to go riding with Miss Ames on the morrow and had no doubt that the father would be there also. Mr. Ames invited Ramsey and Bing-hampton to join the riding party, and while Bing accepted with alacrity, the Earl was obliged to make his excuses.

When the guests made ready to leave, Ramsey exited with them after a cool and formal good night to his fiancée. Lady Pamela was amused at what she felt was jealousy on the Earl's part, but her mother, noting the sardonic look on Ramsey's face, could not feel easy.

CHAPTER SIX

When next Lord Ramsey reached for the brass knocker on Sara's door, at last having been summoned for a sitting, he was almost bowled over by a tall athletic figure. It was Christopher Ames.

"Nemesis!" the Earl muttered.

"Surely not!" laughed Mr. Ames.

"You seem to materialize every way I turn!" Ramsey said in an aggrieved tone.

"I was thinking something along those lines also!" Mr. Ames said with a rueful smile. "I'm afraid to open any door for fear you will be disclosed on the other side. It may turn me into a recluse!"

The Earl acknowledged this sally with a small bow but did not see the same humor in the situation that the American apparently did. The two men exchanged a few polite commonplaces and then parted.

When Ramsey was ushered into the studio he immediately glowered, attributing Sara's sparkling eyes and prettily flushed cheeks to the visitor who had just left. Sara, who had been anticipating this sitting with mingled fear and pleasure, took one look at his dour countenance and immediately became formal and constrained, thus reinforcing his impression.

Without delay Ramsey resumed the pose and Sara took refuge in her work so that the initial awkwardness was soon over. As he watched her absorbed by her painting, he relaxed and eventually an air of contentment pervaded the snug studio. Even occasionally when he would stand up and walk around the room it didn't interfere with the spell. Sara worked in silence and for his part it seemed as if the moment could go on forever without any complaint.

At last a discreet tap on the door was heard and Witherall announced that tea would be ready in a short time. Sara gave a little cry of dismay.

"Good heavens! Is it so late? Forgive me, my lord, I had no idea. You have been uncommonly patient and I must apologize for keeping you so long. Please join me in some refreshment," she added penitently.

Ramsey acquiesced and in a short time they were seated in the cheerful drawing room with its blue and white hangings and elegant rosewood furniture arranged on a Chinese rug of blue, gold and white. The mood established in the studio lingered and they chatted in quiet companionship over tiny sandwiches, hot buttered scones and iced cakes.

At Lord Ramsey's request, she recounted the story of how she had discovered her talents with paints. It was, she told him, on a day when she was filled with ennui. Rummaging in the attic of The Close, she literally stumbled against several oil paintings stacked carelessly against an old chest of drawers. She was a young thing, a mere ten and three, but just one quick look and she knew she'd discovered treasures. She dragged the dusty canvases over to where the sunlight filtered palely through the grimy little window and examined her find. Although a heavy layer of dirt and cobwebs obscured the depth and intensity of color and the forms were rather faintly discernible, she was intrigued enough to persuade Tom-Coachman's son to climb the winding stairs to the second attic and carry her discoveries down to the old nursery.

That day, like the one she first met Jerome, was pivotal in her life. But, of course, she did not make mention of her late husband to Ramsey. She had found five paintings executed by her long dead grandfather Huntley, a man who painted as furiously as he rode to hounds. A man, perhaps so ahead of his time, that his talents went completely unrecognized, especially by his pretty little wife who found her husband's dabbling as embarrassing as his penchant for the bottle. Sara had never known any of her grandparents, her mother's family having been wiped out by a cholera epidemic, and her grandmother Huntley surprising her intimate friends by being so stricken by her husband's lifeless body brought home on a hurdle one fine November day, that she had died on the spot. While Eleanor Huntley's friends could never be sure if despair or relief had hastened her demise, the entire episode furnished gossip for weeks afterward in their small circle.

If the world had not smiled on the strange and uneasy paintings executed by Horatio Huntley, his granddaughter was completely captivated—no insipid pastel renderings of placid pastoral scenes for Sara! She was enchanted by her ancestor's unconventional use of color and the layers of swirling paint which seemed almost to move with a real life of their own; and the way he interpreted what he saw through his own personality filter enchanted her completely.

If hard-pressed to name a favorite, Sara would have had to award the palm to either the sunrise over the hills which had a magical, whimsical and slightly malevolent charm, almost as if a band of mischievous pixies were ready to dance from out behind the trees, or the painting of a barren, windswept Yorkshire moor on a winter's day, which yet hinted at sleeping life waiting only for the call of spring to burst forth into hardy wildflowers and heather-covered vistas all the way to the horizon. Indeed, both paintings were hung on her bedroom wall, and everytime Sara looked at them she saw something more than she had before.

Sara's mother had been rather dismayed by Sara's desire to be instructed in the art of oil painting. "But, my dear, your little water-color sketches are so very pretty. Art and literature were always your strong points!" Mrs. Huntley sighed, thinking of the botched embroidery attempts her daughter had perpetrated with no good grace.

"Oh, but I want to paint in oils, Mama! Oh, do say yes! The colors," she bubbled, "are like jewels, shining with deep inner light." Her rosy cheeks and shining eyes were lit with intensity.

Mrs. Huntley had broached the question to her husband, hoping that he would quash this new start before it snowballed, but Sara's father, who could refuse little he could afford to his only child and dearly-loved daughter, conceded almost immediately. "But," he admonished Sara, most improperly, "no riding hell-bent-for-leather or tippling in taverns, now!" The twinkle in his handsome eye was matched by the one in her own, but Sara managed to retain a most solemn expression on her usually mobile countenance as she offered her solemn word to avoid her grandfather's proclivities.

Thus Sara's life was changed and the Crawleys, a gifted but impecunious brother-and-sister artist pair, came to dwell in the empty rooms on the third floor of The Close and a new world opened up for the young girl. Mornings, Sara and Miss Crawley rode out together if the weather was fine, and afternoons were spent in lessons on line and shape and texture, perspective and balance and composition, and at last, color. These lessons were conducted in the old nursery which was converted into a studio for the use of Sara and her mentors, and the brother and sister would work with her and on their own paintings from lunchtime until tea. Then, much against her will, Sara joined her family in the yellow drawing room while the Crawleys were free to paint until the light failed if they so desired, often taking their meals in the nursery rather than joining the family in the dining room. Enviously, Sara would clean up her brushes and palette and join her parents, while the Crawleys, lost in concentration, would be free to continue at their will.

"How very fortunate you are," Sara once addressed Miss Crawley, "for you can paint all day without interruption, while I am always having to stop just when I am getting exactly the right shading or highlight after fighting with it all afternoon!"

Miss Crawley cocked an eyebrow and exchanged an amused glance with her brother. "Dear child, do you know why we drive ourselves all day like this? We would love to be able to paint and experiment all day, every day! What artist wouldn't! And we are most fortunate indeed, for your father provides us with room and board and a studio and supplies for the happy task of teaching you from our lessons and experience; all we have to do here is paint, but who knows how long this mentorship will continue? Before we were employed by your father, Baldwin worked as a clerk for a merchant twelve hours a day

and I taught art and history to the young ladies of Miss
Underwood's Academy six days a week from eight in the
morning to six in the evening, and who knows how it will
be a year, or a month or a week from now?"

Aghast, Sara exclaimed, "Did you never get to paint?
How terrible!"

"Of course we painted; every evening if we were not
exhausted. But I didn't tell you this to present a picture
of any hardship, Sara; I wanted to tell you that an artist
must use her or his time wisely and this includes the time
spent away from your easel and sketch pads. Right now,
you have a duty to your parents as the daughter of the
house and there are other talents you must develop besides
your art; however, time spent out of the studio is not
wasted time. Look around you, see the quality of light in
a room at different hours, different seasons. Notice how
the lighting or the color of clothing affects the skin tones,
the eye color of the person you are viewing. When you
find a room or a person's dress displeasing, analyze it; is
it the proportion? the color? *What* is it that makes your
artistic eye uncomfortable? And," Miss Crawley continued, her eyes shining with enthusiasm, "when something
is pleasant or looks harmonious you must do the same.
Always, always, use your eyes, use your brain!" The
woman waved her paint brush so sweepingly that it collided with the window frame, bringing her down from her
bandbox. "And now, off to tea you go!"

Sara left the room in a rather subdued mood. Miss
Crawley's words had been a revelation to Sara: "an artist"
was not something one *did*, but something one *was*. Not
just a part of life, but a way of life.

The Earl was charmed with this story. "Do you realize,
ma'am," he commented, smilingly, "that we have been
five hours in each other's company and have not come to
sword points once?"

"You must think me a terrible hornet!" Sara flushed.

"I would like very much to tell you what I think of you," Ramsey began with an almost stern set to his jaw, "but I fear you would not really be interested."

Flustered, Sara said lightly, "Well, it would of course be highly inappropriate in me to encourage myself as a topic of discussion. Tell me, have you seen the new play all of London is talking about? I vow I must be the only person in the city who has not seen it yet."

"*No*, I have not," the Earl replied shortly. A silence which threatened to be awkward ensued.

"Do you go to the Gravestons' ball?" Sara began again with all the civility she could muster.

"Yes," Ramsey replied.

"I am afraid I have tired you out with such a long sitting!" Sara attempted again, asperity creeping into her voice.

"Not at all," her guest answered maddeningly.

"Then perhaps I am boring you to death!" a very provoked Sara exclaimed, her eyes flashing blue fire.

"Now, how can you say that?" the Earl drawled, arching one eyebrow as a slow grin lit his face. "It is just that I am so very contented to sit here and look at you, I find myself quite incapable of making polite conversation."

Before Sara had time to react the double doors to the drawing room were thrown open to admit Augusta and Miss Bensome, who were laden with a number of small parcels. "You must forgive our lateness," Gussie said, "but we have already had tea in any case. Mr. Ames happened upon us with our bundles and not only insisted that he take us up in his carriage but took us to tea since he was afraid I had fagged myself out with shopping so soon after my mishap."

"He is all amiability," the Earl said briefly and made his bow to the ladies.

"Oh, yes!" sighed the normally shy Miss Bensome with a shake of her glossy curls. "And so handsome! There are few people who have suffered as he has under the Cruelty of Fate! And he is so kind and thoughtful of others—" She broke off in embarrassment in the middle of her extravagant litany, taking in the surprised countenances of Sara and the Earl.

"Fulsome praise, but true," Gussie stated. "I have rarely met someone with whom I was so at ease in such short acquaintance."

"And such a romantic figure! Why it is no wonder that Lady Stonemore and Miss Elliot are so taken with him," Amanda added with a stubborn lift of her chim. Like many retiring persons, while she did not speak up often, when she did so it was with staunch courage.

"We will not dispute you, my dear," Sara joined in, noting and interpreting Ramsey's set look as acute boredom.

"Yes," Gussie soothed. "I dare say that half of the eligible young ladies in London have set their caps for him; and those not so young!" she added. "Well, I doubt that most of them would find life in the Wilderness to be their cup of tea."

"Oh, Aunt, surely not the *wilderness!*" Sara chuckled. "Miss Ames herself told me they live on an estate not far from a principal city! Of course, that would not be nearly so romantic a picture for all the young ladies who have developed a *tendre* for the dashing Mr. Ames."

The conversation turned to more general subjects. After a few minutes the disgruntled Earl said his farewells and left the drawing room. He felt uncommonly out of sorts and, if the hapless Mr. Ames had accosted him again on the steps that led to the house in Green Dolphin Street, Ramsey would have had all he could do to prevent himself from giving the American a facer.

Sara had little inclination to analyze the Earl's change in disposition; the strange effect he had on her did not bear investigating. And, since Gussie and Amanda recited in great detail their adventures of the day before, Sara was fully occupied. At last, Amanda bore her off to admire her purchases, and up in the girl's room her worst fears were realized, at least as far as Amanda shopping with Augusta went. The first box Sara saw bore the name of a fashionable modiste who had made her reputation on the *outré* clothes she designed for the demi-monde. One glance at the package was enough to make her wince. A look inside produced a grimace.

Amanda displayed a walking dress of silk bombazine of wide cherry stripes on a cream background with navy piping outlining the puffed sleeves and the very décolleté neckline.

Torn between dismay and laughter, Sara uttered a small choked sound.

"Oh, don't you like it?" Amanda asked, disheartened.

"It's lovely . . ." Sara managed after a deep breath. "But rather . . . rather . . . matronly, don't you think?" she murmured in sudden inspiration.

"Well, now that you say so. It does seem a little . . . dowdy?" Her voice quavered.

"Not dowdy! Perhaps a little too . . . a little too worldly for a young lady making her come-out," she suggested. "Now, if it were only in pink or blue, even a lovely lemon shade . . . and if the neckline were just a very little bit higher, it would be quite the thing."

"Why, there is one almost as you described at Madame Harriette's!" Amanda said. "It was very pale pink and pretty with a charming row of embroidered forget-me-nots at the neck and above the ruffle at the hem. I thought it was simply ravishing."

"But Aunt Augusta told you it was insipid..." Sara finished for her with a smile.

"How did you know?" asked the thunderstruck Miss Bensome.

"I have lived with my aunt for several years now," Sara said affectionately giving her a little hug, "and well I know how easily she forgets that not everyone is of her height or has her style and dash. If you like, I can go shopping with you tomorrow and we can look at that dress you like; I'm in need of some gloves and a shawl for the Gravestons' ball and have put it off for much too long."

Amanda was thrilled by Sara's suggestion.

While Witherall had the most marvelous groom's livery, alas, he had neither horse nor carriage to put to for the ladies. So he hired a hack, making no secret of his displeasure with such an arrangement, and as the creaking carriage moved down Green Dolphin Street, Sara knew she would have to set up her stable again. When she sold her equipage, it had been as much for need of the funds as for lack of use. Now that her portraits commanded such lofty fees, there was no need to begrudge the expense of a few horses and a modest town carriage.

"You must ask Mr. Ames... or Lord Binghampton to look in at Tattersall's, for I have heard that they are both very knowledgeable of horseflesh," Amanda confided. Sara agreed she would consult these gentlemen on the matter when next they met, and the talk turned to whether cream-colored or pale green gloves would look best with a yellow walking dress and whether silk or satin made the most effective half-train.

The day was spent happily in examining ribbons and laces and bows and buckles. Sara purchased some silver lace and several ells of rose silk tissue, as well as some silk stockings and a quantity of soft powder-blue gauze. Amanda bought the pink dress she had seen the previous day, adding a pair of kid gloves and some gilt bows for her shoes. Sara found a lovely shawl of Norwich silk which she purchased as a gift for her aunt, and a set of pearl earrings and pin as a come-out gift for her young friend.

"You are so kind, so good to me," Miss Bensome said between raptures over the dainty pear-shaped drops that dangled from round pearl buttons. She exclaimed they were the very thing to complement the dress she would wear to Lady Graveston's ball later in the week, adding ingeniously that Lord Binghampton had once said nothing became a young lady as did a nice set of pearls.

"What, is Binghampton dropping such indiscreet words into your ear?" Sara teased lightly without thinking.

Amanda blushed rosily. "N...No! You must know he would never be so improper...It is just something I overheard him say...I mean..." she trailed off in confusion.

"I am just funning you, little goose," Sara said kindly and changed the subject; but she was afraid that shy little, dear little Amanda had already given her heart to the gentleman in question. Not that Binghampton was ineligible, for he was kind and personable and surely would be a feather in any girl's cap. He was one of the best matches any fond mama could hope to make for her daughter. Still Sara could not be easy, for she feared Amanda was one who would love not often, but deeply—and Binghampton was clearly stricken with the lovely Miss Ames.

Conveniently forgetting the feelings the Earl of Ramsey stirred in her, Sara felt a pang of sympathy for Amanda and indeed for all young people in the throes of Eros. She congratulated herself for having the superior wisdom not to be seventeen years old and at the mercy of love's whims. Thus it was a shock when they turned the corner of Milsom Street only to see Ramsey sauntering along the sidewalk.

He raised his tall hat and swept the ladies a bow, offering to escort them to the lending library, which was to be their next stop. Since Amanda was too shy to engage the Earl in conversation, that burden fell upon Sara. Ramsey made no effort beyond common civility and he deposited the ladies safely at the library. But, when taking his leave, he added that he hoped he would see them at the Gravestons' and elicited the promise of a dance from each of them. Sara perversely felt a twinge of disappointment and realized that as irritating as she found his comments at times, the day seemed remarkably flat without them!

Had Sara but known, the Earl felt rather flat himself. He had exerted a great deal of restraint just now . . . and all because of an incident that had taken place only a few nights before at Almack's. He'd gone to that esteemed— and in his opinion dull—establishment at the behest of his betrothed. However, when he arrived Lady Pamela and her mother were nowhere to be seen. Spotting the party composed of Augusta Roche, Sara Roche and Miss Bensome, the Earl found his way through the throng to where they stood. He had immediately solicited Sara's hand for the next dance despite her disclaimers of being there to chaperone only, and whisked her out onto the floor.

As they danced, it was apparent at least to one person who knew him well that Ramsey was very taken with the beautiful widow. When he delivered her back to her seat, he lingered a while until the late-arriving Mr. Ames claimed her hand. As he left in search of his cronies, Maria Sefton caught his eye and called him to her side for some private speech.

"Ramsey, my dear, we are such old friends that I know you will forgive me for throwing my oar in. You see, Sara Roche is my cousin and I do not want any more scandal attached to her name. No, wait and hear me out before you protest," she said as the Earl made to speak.

"Since Sara's reemergence into Society, the old whispers have been echoed, but her conduct has been above reproach and the gossips are severely disappointed. If you, a wealthy and titled man possessing a certain reputation with the ladies"—she rapped his knuckles coquettishly with her fan—"make my cousin the object of your attentions, it might cause more talk."

Ramsey, unaware of Sara's history, still had to admit that his friend was right. And, so, he had taken pains to assure that his behavior was most proper in this latest encounter with the lovely artist.

CHAPTER SEVEN

"Really, now!" Sara burst out after one look at With-erall's lugubrious face. "Just because I have a bee in my bonnet to get up before the crack of dawn, there's no need for you to be in such a taking. I didn't rouse you out of your warm bed because I am perfectly capable of making myself a cup of tea without burning down the house, you know."

The butler continued to look like a depressed basset hound. "T'haint fittin'," he asserted, then recalled himself and continued in smooth and proper tones. "If Madame wishes to rise early, Madame should condescend to ring the bell and awaken the staff. If it please, Madame," he added with no good grace.

"Please enact me no Cheltenham tragedies before breakfast!" Sara pleaded, the twinkle in her eye belying the words.

"I promised Mister Jerome I would take care of you, and I will with or without your cooperation," he said politely, but firmly.

"I am sorry, Witherall," Sara said gently, seeing that she had offended him, "but you must remember I am a grown woman and I see no reason to get you out of bed before dawn because I have had an idea I want to try out immediately."

"Would Madame prefer her breakfast in the studio or the morning room?" the "butler" queried in a superior manner, refusing to unbend.

"Oh, in the morning room," she replied in exasperation. Witherall was too like a mother hen clucking over all the ladies of the household, but most especially over her. She redeemed herself by forcing down a coddled egg, two slices of toasted bread with marmalade and a cup of steaming coffee. Then she returned to her studio and worked without pause until luncheon was announced as being imminent by the ever vigilant Witherall.

Although she had begun the Earl's portrait first, Sara was much further along with her representation of Miss Ames. She had used a full-length view portraying Janie in a wooded glade. A dainty doe nestled at her feet and a snowy dove was alight on her outstretched hand. The doe and dove symbolized the young American's naturalness and ease as well as her unaffected innocence. Sara felt she had captured the girl's sweetness and intelligence in the portrait's likeness, as well as her queenly carriage. Still there was something lacking to pull the whole painting together. With a sigh, she cleaned up her equipment and joined Gussie and Amanda at lunch.

"Have some sliced ham," Augusta urged. "You haven't taken enough to keep a sparrow alive."

"That's because Witherall plied me with sufficient food this morning to feed a cavalry regiment!" Sara replied. "You had best look to Amanda, for she is more likely to waste away," she added, noting the listless way the girl was picking at her dish of stewed apricots.

Lost in a dream, Amanda continued to gaze softly into the distance and toy with her food, until Gussie gently laid a hand on her arm.

"Oh, I beg your pardon!" The girl blushed. "I was off wool-gathering," she added unnecessarily.

Gussie chuckled but not too many minutes later found herself the subject of a close look from Sara.

"There seems to be a predilection for wool-gathering this morning; I think you both had better take a repairing lease before you end up in the basket together!" she laughed, her eyes dancing merrily.

"I was . . . just thinking," Gussie said.

"Dear me! Here I had thought you both too fatigued to carry on," Sara teased, "and now I find that you're becoming philosophers."

"My thoughts were not on such a high plane." Gussie smiled. "But I do confess *I* find them quite elevating!" With this mysterious comment and sparkle in her eyes that was quite fetching, Gussie made her excuses and swept out of the room. What, Sara wondered, was her aunt up to now?

But it wasn't too long before she had some clues to help answer the question. The ladies of Green Dolphin Street were going to watch a balloon ascension with Mr. Ames and his daughter. When they pulled up at the doorstep in a very smart black town carriage with elegantly upholstered cushions and squabs of hunter's green with gold piping, it was more than the bright sunshine and crisp breeze that brought a lovely pink tinge to Augusta's cheeks. Sara and Amanda exchanged pleased looks as Mr.

Ames handed Gussie up into the vehicle and solicitously arranged a light blanket over her lap. Janie Ames caught the look between the two women and the corners of her mouth lifted in a dazzling smile. No comment was offered by any of the parties and soon they were on their way, merrily chatting about the coming affairs of the week.

While the others were engaged in conversation, Sara's thoughts were all for Gussie. Watching her eyes shining as Mr. Ames's blond head was tilted close to her aunt's golden one, Sara felt a sharp ache of regret for her self-ishness in keeping her from the gay Society that suited her exuberant personality. She had tried to say something of this to her aunt the previous night, but was told not to be a gudgeon, that she had been as happy in their reclusive existence as she was now in their reemergence into the *haut ton*. Still Sara's reflection was a lowering one.

Her cogitations were interrupted by their arrival at the balloon site from which they would watch the daring adventurers sail off into the clouds. Voices hailed them and in a few moments they were joined by several young bucks of their acquaintance who proceeded to make great cakes of themselves in their attempts to score points with Miss Ames. Lord Binghampton strolled over and began a conversation with Miss Bensome, who was seated a little apart from the others, although not neglected by her companion's high-spirited but well-bred swains.

"Will you permit me to keep you company, Miss Bensome?" He looked especially handsome in a fawn coat with buff breeches and mirror-bright Hessian boots, polished to that gleaming shine with the Beau's famous champagne blacking.

"Oh! Please do! . . . I mean, yes, of course . . . if you like . . ." Amanda stammered in pretty confusion. Bing could not help but notice how her rosy cheeks made her eyes look as blue as hyacinths. In fact, her eyes were so big and so blue that he was quite dazzled and almost forgot himself enough to stare. He was amazed to see how really pretty Miss Bensome was on further acquaintance.

"Would you like a glass of lemonade?" he asked to recover himself.

"Yes, thank you!" Amanda almost whispered as she smiled up at him shyly.

Binghampton seemed to stand a bit taller and straighter as he helped her arrange her shawl and parasol before going off in search of refreshments. When he returned, he was ill-pleased to find that Lord Rutherford, a hardened rake and fortune hunter, was engaged in conversation with Miss Bensome. However, her little heart-shaped face lit up in relief at his return and she turned her blue, blue eyes to him so trustingly that Binghampton almost dropped the glass of lemonade he had procured.

Seeing that he was thwarted, Rutherford took himself off. Miss Bensome did not have enough fortune to tempt him and since she had no coquettish wiles to pass the time in pleasant flirtation, he dismissed her from his mind and went in search of better sport.

Binghampton scowled so ferociously that no one else dared approach them and so he had Amanda to himself for a good length of time. He was surprised and gratified to find that her conversation and ways were as innocently disarming as her appearance. At last the balloon ascension was under way amid many exclamations and shouts and whistles.

Once when the gaily striped balloon was airborne, a sudden change in the air pressure pushed it down. It looked for a moment as if the seemingly tiny wicker gondola would be dashed to the ground with its hapless passengers. Somehow during this time, perhaps after her little squeak of fright, Binghampton's large hand gained possession of Amanda's dainty one in the shouts and confusion before the balloon was safely aloft at last. Only after several minutes did the two realize they were still hand in hand. With blushes, they withdrew their hands and embarked on a fatuous discussion of the weather.

Sara and Miss Ames joined Amanda and Binghampton shortly before they were to return to the carriages. Amanda had stars in her eyes and Sara felt a shadow of worry. The young lord at her side was the same Bing who had dangled after Janie Ames since her debut in London Society. She did not have a very good opinion of the constancy of Binghampton's affections and only hoped that Amanda would not suffer a severe letdown in the weeks to come.

Janie seemed to read her mind, for she gave her arm a little squeeze and told her not to worry, that there would probably come two matches out of the day's companions.

"I think you must know by now," she went on, "that my father has fallen under your Aunt Augusta's spell. You do not object, ma'am, do you?" she asked.

"Why, how could I object when I see them both looking so happy? I have thought there was something coming from that direction."

"Oh, yes!" Janie said, unable to hide a look of relief. "They have been smelling of April and May for this past week."

"Is it as definite as that?" Sara asked.

"Why, I cannot say for your aunt, but I have not seen my father so happy since my mother died. Indeed, I wondered if I could marry and leave him alone in that huge empty house, but yesterday he asked me—oh! not in so many words—if I would be distressed should he want to marry again. I assured him that I would cry for happiness, especially if his intended were a certain someone of my acquaintance. He told me that he would be in a way to ask the 'little lady' soon, if that was the case."

"Little lady?" Sara inquired.

"Well, I cannot be *exactly* certain, you know, but the only woman I have ever heard him call the 'little lady' is Augusta Roche!" Janie laughed for Gussie topped her by a full two inches.

On the return journey, the members of the little party were relatively subdued, wrapped in their individual thoughts. The exceptions were Gussie and Mr. Ames who punctuated the silence with occasional comments, but were for the most part too engrossed in smiling at each other to bother with social etiquette.

Lady Graveston was giving a ball to honor Janie Ames. Gussie was a vision in shades of blue from cerulean to sapphire in her overdress. A matching set of great sapphires and diamonds which would have weighed down a lesser woman was perfect for her statuesque beauty. Amanda was arrayed in a becoming gown of soft white trimmed with apple-blossom ribbons and wore a necklet of seedpearls. She looked altogether angelic. But Sara outshone them. She had taken infinite pains with her toilette and the results showed.

"Oh, Sara!" Miss Bensome gasped. "You look breathtakingly lovely!"

"Yes, my dear," Gussie cried. "You will take the shine out of everyone tonight. Why I feel a positive dowd by comparison!"

Sara demurred, but was gratified to know she was in her best looks. She had no desire to take the shine out of anyone except Pamela Kennerly—and had dressed with that thought in mind! Her gown of rose gauze floated over a deep mauve slip and was trimmed with silver. Sara was delighted with it!

When Witherall, in his groom guise, delivered the ladies to the Gravestons' town house the way was already thronged with carriages. Indeed it looked to be the social event of the Season. Sara, Gussie and Amanda went up the steps and into the foyer where they joined the reception line.

"Do you think Lord Binghampton will be here tonight?" Amanda asked offhandedly as they waited to be presented to their hostess and guest of honor.

"Oh, surely!" Gussie replied unthinkingly. "Anywhere in London that you find Miss Ames you will no doubt find Binghampton!" As she said this she turned and caught a glimpse of Amanda's stricken countenance and added hastily, "I dare say it is just a passing fancy, and for Janie's part I am sure her sentiments toward him are those of friendship only." Amanda brightened perceptibly at this and Gussie and Sara exchanged glances. Gussie had been unaware of Amanda's *tendre* for Binghampton.

"Oh, are you to play the matchmaker?" Sara asked *sotto voce*, recognizing a certain look in Gussie's eye.

"Young people," her aunt whispered, "often need a little nudge from their elders to see what is under their noses. I doubt that Binghampton has truly noticed the little blossom we have been nurturing."

"No, ma'am. And it is such a tender little flower we must take great care that it is not crushed!" Sara said gently.

"Have no fear. A good match may be made in heaven, but there are more than a few that owe their success to Augusta Roche!"

At last they were through the line and made their entrance into the ballroom. Already the heat of the many candles had made the room quite warm, and a footman was opening the long windows that led on to the terrace. In a few moments the ladies were besieged by various males of their acquaintance and their dance cards began to fill. Amanda was a success and did not lack for admirers, but while Lord Binghampton asked Sara to stand up for a waltz with him, he made no move to go over to her shy companion and solicit a dance. Gussie glanced over Amanda's shoulder and saw that a country dance and one waltz, for which the girl had been approved, remained unclaimed. She leaned forward toward Binghampton conspiratorially and whispered, "Quick, my boy! You must rescue my protégée! See that odious Lord Rutherford bearing down on us? He has been making a fatal play to attach her affections. His reputation, you must know, makes him quite unacceptable! If she waltzes with him, the word might be put around that she is fast. And what a tragedy for such a sweet innocent."

Binghampton, having a rather chivalrous streak, besides having been quite taken with Amanda at the balloon ascension, sketched a bow to Gussie and Sara. In a twinkling he swept her out to the dance floor despite her blushing protest that this dance was promised to Mr. Fanton.

The maligned Lord Rutherford continued on down the room, walking past Gussie on his way to the card room, where in fact he had been bound all along. Sara watched Amanda dancing happily in Binghampton's arms and turned to her aunt with a questioning look. "Now, just how did you arrange that, ma'am?"

Gussie did not deign to reply, but favored Sara with a very mischievous smile. She turned to the topic of the perfectly frightful yellow-green gown with overmantle that Mrs. Barnette had chosen to wear.

When the dance ended Lord Binghampton restored Amanda to her friends and claimed Sara for the country dance about to start.

"A taking little thing, your Miss Bensome," he said as they took their place on the floor.

"Yes," Sara smiled. "Amanda is a dear, gentle creature and only wants a little town-bronze to rid her of her shyness. If she were a trifle less reserved, I believe she would be one of the hits of the Season. So very pretty-mannered and sweet-natured." Here they parted in the steps of the dance and Sara was pleased to have dropped some phrases complimentary of her young friend into Binghampton's ear. She was therefore gratified presently to have him resume the conversation when they were brought together again.

"Not my place, but just a word of caution, ma'am. Wouldn't do to encourage Rutherford to dangle after her. Little thing's not up to snuff yet. No offense, ma'am!" He paused and again apologized for interfering where he had no right, ending in rather incoherent remarks indicating he realized Amanda's hostesses would see she got along all right.

Sara adjured him to be easy in mind, telling him she was grateful to know Amanda had a friend interested in her welfare for the girl was such a trusting innocent.

"Oh, true, ma'am," he responded. "A mere babe in the woods!" He indicated he would ask to take Miss Bensome in to supper before Rutherford or "others of his ilk" might claim the honor.

Sara was unaware of the part Amanda's blue eyes played in his plan, but she and Gussie were delighted to see him hover near Amanda in his new role of protector. They were not the only ones to notice Binghampton's gallantry, as he discovered when he found himself beside his sister while Amanda stood up with Mr. Taryton.

"What eccentric tastes you are developing, Binghampton! First you make a brown Indian the object of your attentions," cooed Lady Pamela, "and now a little mouse."

"Better a mouse than a shrew," he said coolly and strolled off. As he went in search of the punch bowl he almost collided with Ramsey in the doorway.

"Tell you what, Ramsey! Don't do it!" he muttered

darkly. "You'll never have a day's peace again. Take my advice before it's too late."

"I very likely would, if only I knew what you are raving about!" Ramsey declared. "Are you overwrought? It's much too early to be in your cups, and I must say you don't look foxed."

"Not foxed! Women!" Binghampton said cryptically.

"But of course," Ramsey laughed. "Now all is made clear! And since that is settled, perhaps we can go in search of some of Graveston's very excellent brandy."

"Just so I'm in time to take Miss Bensome in to supper," Bing stated.

"What, have you deserted the lovely Diana? Or were you merely behindhand with your solicitation?"

"Neither. It's that Miss Ames has so many admirers vying for her favor. And Miss Bensome, being just up from the country and all, needs someone to take her best interests to heart."

"I see!" said Ramsey with a knowing look.

"No, dash it all! It's not what you think, Edward. My interest in Miss Bensome is purely brotherly."

"Why, I disremember you ever being worried about how your sister got along in Society!" The Earl laughed.

"Don't get me started!"

The two men went off together to find the brandy and relax away from the crowded ballroom. Binghampton made his reappearance in good time to escort Amanda in to supper.

"I thought you might not remember," she told him shyly.

"Good Lord! A fine fellow you must think me!"

"Oh, no indeed!" Amanda exclaimed, her eyes bright with a sudden sting of tears. "My unfortunate tongue! I know you are all that's proper. Pray forgive me!"

"What a little pea-goose you are. I was just roasting

you, you know." Binghampton smiled, taking her little hand and giving it a squeeze before tucking it under his own.

With her cheeks flushed and eyes sparkling Amanda was so lovely that several guests were heard to remark on the little Bensome's very good looks this night.

Mr. Ames had engaged to take Gussie and Sara into supper and was about to stroll off with the ladies when Ramsey descended on them.

"Oh, no you don't! You cannot be so greedy! I will pirate away one of these fair ladies." Without further ado he detached Sara from the arm of her erstwhile escort and led her away before she could remonstrate with him. An indignant Lady Pamela was led in by a happy Mr. Fanton.

Sara thought they would sit down with her aunt and Mr. Ames, but the Earl bore her off to where Miss Bensome sat with Binghampton. Flatly, he stated he had seen quite enough of the American and did not wish to have Mr. Ames's face before him through supper also.

After their refreshment, Binghampton suggested they take a turn on the terrace. Sara felt there could be no harm in this and as the evening was warm some fresh air sounded pleasant. They ran into four young friends of Binghampton's and joined forces.

Although the moon was low on the horizon, the starlight was bright enough to see the garden paths clearly. The group wandered through the pleasant shrubbery and down to the more formal terraces at the side of the Gravestons' elegant town house. Sara stopped to exclaim over the beauty of some fragrant roses, adding that they reminded her of the garden at The Close when she was a child. "It was the most beautiful garden I have ever seen!"

"I would like you one day to see the gardens at Ramsey Park," the Earl said to her. "They were designed by a friend of mine and are acknowledged to be very fine in an unusual sort of way."

"I somehow imagine that nothing associated with you would be of a usual sort, my lord," Sara replied before she could guard her tongue.

"Perhaps that is why I find *you* so intriguing, madame, for *you* are very much out of the common way!" He smiled down at her warmly.

Flustered by her own remark, as well as his admiring glance, Sara retreated into a camouflaging coolness of manner and changed the subject abruptly.

"Do you think this fine weather will hold, sir? We are planning to ride out with Miss Bensome to the country tomorrow, and I do hope the day will be clear."

"Now, that is precisely what I mean! Any other woman of my acquaintance would have responded to my comment with an arch look and asked what I meant, but you turn into a Frost Queen and begin spouting inanities about the weather."

Ruffled, Sara attempted to persist with her diversionary tactics. "Well, of course, you may not care about the weather, but I am sure I don't want to take a soaking if it turns wet."

"Hang the weather!" the Earl exclaimed impatiently, blocking the path so that Sara could proceed no farther. Turning around quickly, she noticed for the first time that they had become separated from the rest of their party. She had thought the young people just a few feet behind them, and Ramsey had done nothing to disabuse her of this notion. She uttered a small sound of dismay and attempted to return up the terrace steps, but was stopped by a firm grip on her arm. Smiling almost fiercely, the Earl pulled her into the deep shadows of a leafy tree.

"Are you afraid of me?" he asked softly.

Sara made a rather inarticulate reply and tried politely

to remove his hand from her arm. "No, of course not," she finally said. It was not at all the thing to be seen alone in the garden with a man, much less to be seen struggling in a most undignified manner.

"That is much better," the Earl smiled, not loosening his grip.

"We must return to the ballroom at once. Pray release my arm," Sara said in her most formal manner.

"What? Are you afraid of what people might say? Why, I'm alone in the studio with you for hours! I believed you a woman who didn't put great emphasis on what others might think."

Piqued, Sara answered, "I am not afraid of you and I am not overly concerned with others' opinions. I will return to the ballroom because *that* is what I *wish* to do!"

"Do you?" The Earl asked softly, reaching his other arm around her waist and pulling her hard against him. "I think perhaps you *are* afraid of me . . . or at least afraid I might do this."

He bent his head with great deliberation and kissed her full on the mouth. He was ardent, demanding, and Sara was thrown into confusion. At last he lifted his lips from hers and he looked down on her with great tenderness in his eyes, holding her tightly as she swayed against him.

"Oh, Sara!" he breathed, gathering her close to his chest and kissing her at first gently, and then so fervently that her lips felt bruised.

So great an impact did his kiss and the strength of his encircling arms have upon her, she yielded herself up to the moment, her arms sliding up his strong chest to his neck, as if to embrace him. She had the sensation that she was melting into his body, her breasts crushed into the warmth of his chest, his thighs pressed hard against her.

Then, a small sound nearby brought her to her senses and she began to struggle to free herself. Reluctantly,

Edward released her. Before he could say a word, she turned on her heel, fled up the terrace and in through the open windows, leaving him to call her name softly in despair. Angry at his own rashness, Ramsey stormed into the house, but though he searched the ballroom and the small parlors he couldn't find her. He cursed the fatal impetuousness of the Ramsey family. Would he never learn to guard against his sudden impulses?

CHAPTER EIGHT

A quick look through the rooms on the ground floor of the town house produced only one that was lighted; a small fire flickered cheerfully in the grate, casting a dim glow over the walls of the library. She sat in a leather wing chair. At first she could only go over and over the events in the garden, remembering Ramsey's words and actions. A lock of hair had tumbled down to her shoulder, and she brushed it away as she remembered the feel of his arms about her, the warmth of his lips on hers. Slowly, she raised the back of her hand and touched it to her mouth where his kisses had been pressed. Her thoughts were in total disorder.

A sound at the door made Sara peek around the edge of the chair. Two figures were visible just inside the door-way, a man and woman locked in an embrace. She won-

dered if it would be better to break the silence with some
discreet little sound or to stay perfectly still and hope the
amorous couple would depart quickly without learning
they had an audience. At that moment, she felt in tune
with anyone stealing a few seconds of bliss in a lover's
arms. Realizing how she would have felt if someone had
come upon her in the Earl's embrace in the garden earlier,
she decided that silence was the most tactful recourse.

After a few kisses the anonymous sweethearts gave no
indication of leaving and Sara grew agitated with herself
for not making her presence known immediately. She
wondered idly who they were—not their names or ranks.
Were they star-crossed by reason of position in life, a lack
of fortune? Or were they married unhappily to others for
convenience, as was so often the case, and now finding
a few minutes of illicit happiness? Her questions were
soon answered. She heard a man's voice say with tender
sincerity, "You have made me the happiest man alive!"

"When you look at me that way," Christopher Ames
declared to the woman in his arms, "I feel I could move
mountains, I could hold Niagara Falls back with one
hand."

"Ah, you are so bold and fiery. I think that's what made
me love you from the first! But whatever *is* Niagara Falls?"
Augusta Roche teased, her voice husky.

"Why, Niagara is just the place to take you on our
wedding trip! It's a huge gorge at the precipice of the
Niagara River in America. Like nothing you've ever seen!
The foaming waters cascade over an enormous shelf of
crescent-shaped rock down hundreds of feet into the seething cauldron below. The ground trembles for miles around,
and as one approaches the falls from a distance, the low,
whispering sound increases until it's a giant's roar that
reverberates through one's bones. The spray whips upward
making rainbows against the sky at every turn."

"Oh, I am marrying a poet!" Gussie applauded. "It sounds a most awesome sight, and I would love to see it . . . although I must declare that I'd find a pond exciting in your company."

"What a woman you are!" Mr. Ames exclaimed, taking his intended once more into his strong arms.

Sara sat paralyzed as embarrassment warred with her delight that Gussie and the American were making a match of it. While Sara wondered again if she should make her presence known, Gussie reluctantly tore herself from her lover's arms. Announcing her intention of seeking out Sara to announce the engagement, she whirled away.

Sara curled back in the chair, hoping that Mr. Ames would leave so she could "appear" in the ballroom to receive Gussie's confidences. It was not fated to be. After a few seconds of musing silence the tall American strolled over toward the fireplace. Sara stood up and began to apologize.

"Indeed, I didn't mean to overhear. I was sitting here lost in thought and didn't hear you and my aunt come in. Pray excuse my appalling lack of courtesy!"

"My dear," Mr. Ames said, "put yourself at ease. I realize you were caught in a most difficult quandary." He took her hand and smiled his open smile. "I only hope you aren't displeased by what was disclosed just now."

"How could I be displeased with such a joyous announcement?" Sara replied. "I am so happy to see Gussie glowing like the sun these days. And knowing that your dear daughter also holds her in affection makes it all perfect. I wish you happy, sir!"

Mr. Ames took Sara's small hand in his large one and smiled with relief. "I hope you won't miss the little lady too severely. We have already discussed this and want you to know we would like you to make your home with us!"

"Thank you," Sara said with a twinkle in her eye, "but

I think I would be considerably *de trop* at this time in your life. Besides, I am kept occupied by my painting, so don't fear that I will pine away for lack of employment!"

"If not now, perhaps later you will change your mind. And I am not merely being polite, as I fear you think, for we would clearly love to share our home with you. At least think about coming to America soon," he added.

Sara responded by reaching up to plant a congratulatory kiss on Mr. Ames's cheek. Unfortunately, Ramsey poked his head through the open doorway of the library, only to see her reach up to embrace another man. A swift look took in the scene, and, as the Earl recognized the other man, he thrust himself into the room with an oath.

"So this is why you run from my embraces!" he said, charging upon the couple. His swing caught the American off guard causing him to stumble back upon the mantel. In a trice Mr. Ames caught the Earl, whom he supposed to be either drunk or mad, with a swift blow to the chin. Ramsey fell against the side of the chair, changing to a defensive stance, but the American didn't follow up his advantage.

"Remember you are in the presence of a lady!" Mr. Ames said with quiet force just as Augusta came in.

"Are you both mad?" she pronounced scathingly as she rushed across the room.

The Earl belligerently whispered in an undervoice to the American, "Appoint your seconds, sir, and mine will call round in the morning." He bowed stiffly to the ladies and made his exit.

Trembling, Sara threw herself upon Gussie's generous bosom and broke into sobs. Gussie looked at her fiance in amazement.

"What on earth has transpired?" she asked.

"It's too long a tale, I think, to discuss here," Mr. Ames said decisively. "I will order the carriage sent round and escort you two home. I will return for Janie and Miss Amanda after you are settled, and Lady Granville will look after them till then."

Gussie comforted Sara but didn't ask any further questions, secure that her intended would take care of everything in the proper time. She soothed Sara, who sobbed as if her heart would break, and then helped her pin up the loose strands that had fallen from her coiffure.

"Come, my dear. Christopher will get our wraps and we'll go home immediately." The American returned on the tail of these words and escorted the two ladies to his carriage, reassuring them that he had sought out their hostess and given the excuse of a sudden indisposition. As they drove through the London streets, Sara closed her eyes and turned her head toward the lavishly upholstered squabs. She tried to quiet her mind. By the time they reached Green Dolphin Street she had succeeded to the point that she felt empty and dull inside and probably would not have noticed a regiment of cavalry parading by.

Streaming through the thin curtains, the early-morning light awakened Sara, and she stretched sluggishly and yawned before memory of the night's events returned. She lay very still and thought of the words Ramsey had said and of the way his hard body had felt pressed tight against hers. Flushing, she remembered how she'd reached up and responded to his lovemaking. A hot fire radiated from the pit of her stomach down her legs and up into her chest.

Suddenly she was overwhelmed with physical longing such as she hadn't known since the difficult times after Jerome died. She clenched her teeth as the ache rose in her loins and spread through her veins like a wildfire out of control. Grabbing the pillow, she held it against her breasts as if she held Ramsey crushed to her body again in an attempt to assuage the sensation, then flung it away and pounded the mattress with her fists, kicking her feet against the sheets.

Why, oh why, she thought, wasn't she a man? A man would never have to know such longing. He could always find some woman willing to share her favors, if not for love at least for pleasure...or money. But what could a woman do? Society permitted so much to a man. Where was there any relief for Sara and the women like her?

She leaped out of bed and went to the window, flinging back the curtains. She opened the window and breathed in the morning air, trying to keep her thoughts away from her physical need. Looking down, she saw the kitchen maid at the house next door indulge in a passionate kiss with the groom from across the way. Sara shut the window with a bang, not even noticing that she had startled the young lovers.

"Why am I this way?" she cried aloud as she prowled the carpeted floor. "Why do I have these feelings? These needs?" She remembered how shocked Jerome had always been by her actions and reactions when making love. Once when he was dressing Sara had come up behind him and slid her arms up under his shirt, holding herself tightly against him while she stroked his chest lightly with her fingers. He pulled away from her in disgust and commanded her to stop behaving like a hussy.

"Oh, Jerome!" she had cried, "Why do you always have to be so poetic and high-minded? I feel like some princess in a tower, untouched and untouchable! Why can't we hold each other, touch each other, lie in each other's arms like we used to!"

"Our love must be a temperate and undefiled love; a pure love, not like the coarse groping and coupling of peasants!" Jerome said violently. "Every time...every time we make love, I remember that I took you before we were man and wife. *I*, who had promised to protect you!"

he summed up bitterly as he pulled on his jacket and left their bedroom.

It seemed that the more Sara needed his touch, his embrace of love, the more Jerome made himself aloof. She knew she disappointed him terribly. Jerome had wanted to be the gentle knight, protecting his lady and worshiping her from afar; but Sara was a woman with a woman's needs for love, as well as tenderness and affection. Her intrinsic womanliness forced Jerome to acknowledge, at least from time to time, the urges of his masculinity. As the early years of their marriage passed, he turned from her physical magnetism as a searcher for the Grail would from worldly corruption— Sara had become his Lilith.

Still, she had found herself loving Jerome and feeling somehow wanton and sinful because of the natural urgings of her young body. As he withheld himself on a physical level, he began to withdraw emotionally, abhoring his responsiveness to Sara's beauty and sweetness. At the age of nineteen, she had spent untold nights alone, weeping in frustration but unable to change her nature.

Now, she felt as she had then. It was a shock to realize that if Ramsey were here, right now, in her room, she would welcome his kisses and more! Flinging herself once more upon the bed, she cried softly into her pillow until she fell asleep again.

In her dreams she was back in the garden with Ramsey, holding him close as his hands carefully unbuttoned her bodice and explored the softness of her body. Then suddenly they were lying in front of the fire in the library at the Gravestons' town house and she was astonished to find herself naked in the firelight. She dreamed that he whispered words of love and when at last he took her she felt herself falling giddily through time and space only to see him stand up and adjust his clothing while he eyed her coldly. "Wanton!" the Lord Ramsey of her dream shouted, and she awoke to find herself tangled in the sheets of her narrow, lonely bed.

Tired and aching, she dressed and went down to breakfast where her wise and sympathetic Aunt Augusta managed to divert Amanda's conversation with recollections of the ball so that Sara's silence went virtually unnoticed. Since Amanda was engaged to go on a shopping expedition with Miss Ames, Gussie and Sara were left alone for the rest of the morning.

They had retired to the solar with the early post when Gussie plunged in.

"My dear, would you like to talk about it?" she asked carefully, noting Sara's shadowed eyes.

"I think perhaps Lord Ramsey had imbibed too freely," Sara said, trying to pass it off lightly.

"Then he must still be foxed," Gussie retorted with asperity, "for he sent a note to Christopher naming his seconds and asking Christopher's seconds to call upon them soonest."

"Good Lord, no!" Sara cried.

"Don't worry, dear," Gussie went on, "this all happened while you were still abed this morning. Christopher came by to let us know that all is smoothed over. He went to Ramsey and most correctly pointed out that the right of challenge belonged to *him* as the injured party, *not* to Ramsey! And since Christopher has no intention of doing anything so foolish and is truly the most amiable man in the world, everything was settled nicely in all events."

"Thank heaven for that!"

"Yes. It would never do to have a breach between my husband-to-be and..." Here Gussie hesitated, changed her mind and went on. "...and someone sitting for one of your portraits."

Sara was struck for a moment. So caught up was she

in her relationship with the Earl that she had not considered, not even *thought* of the portrait.

"Excuse me, I must send off a note at once, Aunt!" She declared. She hurried to the morning room, only to sit staring blindly out the window for the better part of forty-five minutes. At last she took pen in hand and scribed:

> Madame Roche regrets that all further sittings for the portrait must be postponed indefinitely as she is called to the country for a period of time.

She read this through, tore it up and castigating herself for a chicken-heart, began again:

> I think it would be best to cancel the sittings for the portrait. I do not feel able to complete it under the circumstances.

This too, she tore into pieces, she was wracking her brain for a better way to phrase her thoughts when Witherall opened the door, announcing, "The gentleman who waited, otherwise known as Lord Ramsey, sixth Earl of Ramsey, Viscount Blanshaw..."

Any further titles were cut off abruptly as the Earl removed the door handle from Witherall's grasp and firmly shut the door in his astonished face.

"Your servant, madame." He bowed, his eyes searching her countenance.

Sara sat very straight, her face drained of all color, and Ramsey frowned slightly at her apparent unease.

"I have come," he began formally and rather stiffly, "to beg your pardon for my uncivilized behavior last evening and to ask your forgiveness for the distress I have no doubt I have caused you."

Her cheeks, so pale a moment before, were suffused

with a fiery blush. She found that she could not meet his eyes, and turned her head slightly in embarrassment.

"Don't turn from me," Ramsey burst out. "I grant I have given you every reason to do so! I was prepared to find myself barred from your door and could not blame you if you had done so. Can we not . . . pretend . . . that last night didn't happen and proceed as we were?" He made no move to enter further into the room, but stood watching her.

Sara looked up and her heart wrenched to see him standing there so tall and handsome, his eloquent eyes burning amber as he looked at her. With a deepening flush she remembered her thoughts of the morning which only increased her discomposure.

Ramsey bowed and said regretfully, "I see I have offended you beyond pardon. Good day, madame. I will importune you no further." He turned to leave.

"Wait!" Sara exclaimed, still separated from him by the distance of the room. She paused as the Earl turned around and watched her thoughtfully.

"There are only one or two sittings left to finish the portrait . . . I have never left a work unfinished . . . perhaps we could...resume the sittings," she ended all in a rush. Ramsey's glowing look and elegant bow almost made her regret the impulse but there was nothing to be done for it. He left with the agreement that he would keep his appointment on the morrow at two in the afternoon.

After he left, Sara's mood was lightened considerably although she resolutely avoided thinking of the Gravestons' ball or of Ramsey's morning call and apology. She was afraid to analyze her feelings—even more afraid to attempt to identify the motives which had prompted the Earl. She would ignore the whole episode.

Gussie said no more on the subject that day. As Mr. Ames and his daughter joined the three ladies for dinner,

Sara was too busy to spend any time repining. The little party dined on roast squab removed with veal Florentine and dishes of peppered squash and brussels sprouts. After a dessert of meringues and cherry tartlets, the ladies made ready to retire to the drawing room, leaving Mr. Ames in solitary splendor to enjoy a glass of port and a cigar. This he would not do, however.

"Why should I be condemned to sit alone, while I only long to be cozy with such charming ladies?" he demanded, adding, "of course, if you need a respite from my company . . . ?" This was pronounced with a most forlorn look, quite contrary to his engagingly lopsided grin.

The ladies denied any wish to be quit of his society, and all removed to the drawing room. Augusta engaged her swain in a game of chess, urged on by Amanda who had learned to play only since she joined the Mesdames Roches, but had developed quite a flair for strategy. This left Janie with the opportunity to involve Sara in conversation, ostensibly on the pretext of discussing the forthcoming wedding.

"Oh, Sara, I do hope you will change your mind and come to America!" she said after they had talked a while. "It is so open and free and exciting. Although I have come to love England, I must admit I'll be glad to be home again!"

"Are you so sure that you are going home with your father?" Sara said with a smile. "I had thought we might make an Englishwoman of you yet, for I declare you'll break many hearts if you leave."

"Well, it might break *my* heart to stay too long," Janie said with a chuckle, "for Paul MacAllister has written twice a week since we've been here, and he swears he'll come fetch me over his shoulder if I'm not returned by September!"

"Then you've made a decision!" Sara observed, then gave Janie a hug.

"Yes. Paul has always been the only one for me, but my father wanted me to be quite sure. I must admit the Season has done me much good but I have never wanted anything so much as I want to be home with Paul. Please, I beg you, keep my confidence in this."

Sara was silent for a moment, remembering the days when she had wanted nothing more than to have Jerome by her side forever. She realized that Janie, almost three years older than she had been at the time of her runaway marriage with Jerome, was much more mature and probably had a much more realistic idea of the meaning of marriage than she had had at the same age. Janie had certainly gained in poise and confidence since her arrival for the glittering London Season.

Almost as if reading her thoughts, Janie said, "I was so very shy and unsure of myself just a few weeks ago. And, though I was well received here, I still felt large and gangling and awkward. Then I met your Aunt Augusta! She carries herself so elegantly. I learned a woman could be tall yet still feminine and delicate seeming. What an inspiration she has been to me!" Her eyes were shining. "After Lady Linville's ball, my father said of her, 'she glides across the floor with the beauty and majesty of a yankee clipper.' It was then I knew how smitten he was, for you must know his clipper ships are his pride and joy!"

"I think there are two who must come before even his ships in your father's affections," Sara laughed merrily.

It was quite late when the father and daughter took their leave, and she dropped off to sleep quickly after the exhausting events of the long day.

Early the next morning she was up and at her easel before the pained Witherall, who scowled and threatened to return "to the boards" if she continued not allowing him to look after her in "a manner befittin' ha lidy." She did, however, sooth his ruffled feathers by partaking of a huge breakfast!

In her studio once more, she studied Ramsey's portrait. The pose was set and the background filled in. It needed only the final touches, the nuances of expression and personality to be crystallized on the canvas. Sara sighed and stepped back, eyeing the picture in satisfaction. She tried to convince herself that the only reason she wanted to finish the sittings was the painting and not the subject.

She could see that this portrait was her best, perhaps her masterpiece. The commanding presence of the subject, she knew, had given her the basis for the work, but she had reached a new peak of subtlety and harmony in line and color. She wondered how he would react to her interpretation.

The background of the painting was dark-textured emerald with gleams of gold, and if one looked closely the jagged shadows might give the impression of a dragon with wide arching wings extended, but a more casual onlooker would be impressed by the power and energy portrayed by the artist. In the portrait, the Earl sat calmly, yet Sara had succeeded in capturing the tension and lithe muscularity that rippled beneath exquisitely tailored clothing. Near Ramsey's right hand there rested a jewel-encrusted sword, the blade wickedly bright against his side, but the sword was ensnared by a vine that twined around both the blade and the hilt. The face in the portrait, although not fully detailed yet, showed a stern gentleness that formed a striking contrast with the imperious pose of head and wide shoulders. Only the eyes and firm-lipped mouth were still little more than slashes on the canvas.

Well, Sara thought, only one or two more sittings and the portrait would be finished. Instead of the rush of energy and enthusiasm she usually experienced at this point in a

painting, though, Sara had a nagging feeling of dissatis-
faction. She resolutely ignored it.

Later, in a comfortable chat with Amanda and Gussie,
she asked if all the wedding plans had been made.

"Since Christopher and I tumbled into love and became
affianced so quickly" —she paused, blushing like a girl—
"my darling American has promised to give me a proper
courtship. Although I *was* able to talk him out of sere-
nading me like the Spaniards do, since we don't have a
balcony," she added with a twinkle.

"Oh, but how romantic that would be!" Amanda exclaimed.

"Yes, but how unfortunate for the neighbors," Sara
teased.

"Well, we shall see," said the beaming Augusta, "for
Christopher is a most unusual, a most original man!" This
was proved shortly afterward when the house on Green
Dolphin Street was virtually inundated with flowers. There
poured a steady stream of great bouquets as well as dainty
nosegays in silver paper. A river of roses flowed to Gussie. They were in every conceivable color from white to
pink through pale yellow and peach to the whole family
of crimson and scarlet. Each bouquet was accompanied
by a card with an inscription: "For the loveliest Rose."
"To my beautiful Rose." All, of course, in Christopher's
distinctive hand. With both her aunt and Amanda in transports, Sara was hard put to decide which was the more
delighted.

CHAPTER NINE

Two o'clock came and Sara was once more in her studio when Lord Ramsey was announced. He was very formal and correct which relieved her mind considerably—while managing to nettle her at the very same time. She maintained an aloof and formal air except when his head began to drift slightly to the right.

"You must hold your pose! It is critical at the moment," she said, more strongly than she had intended. "Lift your chin a quarter inch and turn your head back this way ever so slightly." The Earl complied but in a few minutes Sara again exclaimed that he had altered the pose. "Lift your chin, please. Oh dear, no, not that much!"

"Show me," Ramsey responded smoothly, his eyes shining.

"I am full of paint."

The two stared at each other for a few seconds, then the Earl relented, and dropping his gaze, resumed the proper position. The sitting went on without further incident and if Sara's hand trembled a little when she brought his firm, determined mouth to life in the painting, all went smoothly until she called a halt.

"Are you done, then?" Ramsey asked in some surprise, for the sitting was far shorter than usual.

"No," Sara admitted, "I'm just having some difficulty with my concentration today. Rather than struggle, I'd prefer to finish at another sitting." There was no way she could admit that the thought of looking him in the eye for an extended period of time completely undid her! Whenever she caught that smoldering golden glance a small shock went through her body making her feel as confused and gauche as a chit in the schoolroom.

"I do wish you would let me see the portrait. I find it difficult to keep my curiosity in bounds."

"I'm hampered by the subject viewing the unfinished work. And it is, after all, only one more sitting." Sara laughed.

"Very well." Ramsey rose. "Will I see you tonight at Princess Metzenberger's drum?"

"No, we are engaged to see the fireworks at Vauxhall Gardens tonight with...with friends," Sara answered, leaving Ramsey in no doubt as to the identity of those "friends." Although his firm mouth thinned a little, he made no comment and left after making arrangements for the final sitting.

Mr. Ames joined the three ladies for tea and the talk was light and congenial over scones, lettuce sandwiches and frosted tea cakes. Sara had announced that the engagement would catch many by surprise, since no one was aware that a courtship had been in progress.

"Well, we Americans are a fast-moving and spontaneous lot. And when we find a good woman, why we don't wait around!" Christopher laughed. "We just throw them over our saddles and ride off."

"Like Lochinvar!" Augusta beamed. "But I still must have a proper courtship, don't you think? Merely to set an example for these young people, you understand."

"If you are unconventional enough to agree to an engagement before the courting, the least I can do is see you're properly wooed!"

"Oh," Amanda exclaimed. "How very romantic! Shall you send sonnets and sing serenades beneath her balcony?"

"Well, not the serenades, perhaps," Christopher said, a merry glint in his eyes. "I'm told you don't really have a proper balcony."

"But Peregrine serenaded Julia last week, and she doesn't have a balcony either, just a garden." Amanda sighed.

"There you are, my dear," Gussie teased her intended. "I'm sure that you will be able to think of something."

At this point the American was grinning widely and the sparkle in his eye made Sara wonder what the enterprising gentleman would conjure up for his lady's amusement. To see them in the same room was a revelation. Their eyes sought one another's across the table or across the room and their happiness was almost palpable. Sara ruefully acknowledged to herself that it was a strange feeling to be the chaperone for Gussie after all these years!

"Have you set the exact date for the happy event yet?" she inquired of the lovebirds.

"Do you think me too elderly for a June bride?" Gussie asked archly, knowing the effect her words would have.

"June!" Miss Bensome squealed with delight as Sara echoed her pleased surprise. "Why, June is almost upon us."

"We'll be married by special license June fourteenth

at St. George in Hanover Square," Christopher announced, eyeing Sara carefully. "Then we'll tour the countryside and take a jaunt over to Paris for a while before returning to London. That will give us some time to see everyone and settle arrangements for America."

If Sara felt any dismay at the thought of losing Gussie so quickly, she hid it well in her cheerful manner.

"Well, we will have to go shopping for your bride-clothes as soon as possible. What great fun that will be!" Sara said to her aunt.

"Oh, if only America weren't all the way across the Atlantic!" Gussie smiled affectionately at her niece.

"Why, then it wouldn't *be* America, would it!" Sara laughed bravely, but a small heavy weight settled around her heart. Not to see Gussie, perhaps for years!

As if reading her thoughts, Mr. Ames again invited Sara to join them in Virginia, or to at least come on an extended visit of several months. He also opened the invitation to include Amanda who, while gratified by the offer, found the whole idea rather overwhelming.

Later Sara went into her small sitting room to go over some household accounts but found she couldn't keep her attention fixed properly. So many changes were occurring in her life—and so rapidly! A short time ago nothing occupied her mind before dropping off to sleep at night except thoughts of the current painting in progress, or a new book she was reading and discussing with Gussie ...or some affectionate amusement at her aunt's latest enthusiasm. Things had been on a very even keel, and if in retrospect a bit boring, well Sara had not really noticed. Now, however, she felt restless and dissatisfied.

"It must be pure selfishness at Gussie's leaving me. What a greedy little beast I've become!" she castigated herself aloud. At this moment she was far more ready to claim a vice than to look into her heart and address the root of the problem. She closed her account book with a sigh, sat back and shut her eyes for a moment. Instantly her mind was flooded with an image of Lord Ramsey's handsome, slightly mocking face. The image was so real she could feel his amber-dark eyes boring into her, making her accept the facts she had so resolutely ignored. Any day when she did not meet him somewhere was curiously flat and dull, leaving her cross as crabs. Any time she knew she would be seeing him, she walked on air and the gloomiest day seemed filled with light. But when indeed she was with him her tongue was either tied in knots or dagger-sharp and she felt awkward and shy. If he smiled, her spirits rose. If he frowned—or, heaven forbid, ignored her—she was utterly cast down.

"Damn him!" Sara cried out softly. "He has destroyed all my peace!" The sound of her own voice caught her up. "After all," she muttered, "it isn't his fault that a woman of my age acts like a silly chit because of him. He's certainly a very accomplished flirt . . . and his address is of the best . . . and I can't take him to task because the words he says or actions he takes have rendered me completely foolish on his account. An experienced Society matron would flirt back outrageously, enjoying every minute of it, but never, never taking him seriously! Well, he has an affianced wife and at least one mistress . . ." She remembered the red-haired bit-of-muslin from the milliner's shop. "And I will put him out of my mind! I daresay once the portrait is finished and Amanda is successfully launched I will probably never see him again." This last thought, while making her feel nobly determined, brought her no comfort at all. In fact she felt decidedly worse for it!

By dinner time Sara was in even lower spirits. The attractions of Vauxhall Gardens and a fireworks display left her unmoved. They dined in the formal dining room and Augusta looked around with satisfaction at the transformation in the cozy room. The white-painted wainscoting and the new pale rose wallpaper picked out in gilt highlighted the lusters of the chandelier which cast rainbow lights across the place settings and splashed dancing colors on the ceiling. The new chairs with their classical style and straw-colored satin seat covers added the completing touch as they matched the new swag-hung draperies at the windows.

Augusta heaved a contented sigh. "Could one have guessed a few short weeks ago how altered our lives would be?"

"No, indeed!" Sara replied, with equal strength but less equanimity.

"And mine!" Amanda smiled prettily. "All thanks to my two kind benefactresses," she added. "Why I would be sitting in the drawing room with dear Mother and Father and Grandmother and Ninian and Blanche and Marcus and Ruth," she said, naming her siblings. "We would sew while Father read to us until nine o'clock when the tea cart would be brought in and then it would be off to bed. I must confess that after keeping Society hours in London, it will be dreadfully flat to keep country hours again."

"Perhaps you will not be returning to the country so soon, or at least only for the off season and the hunting," Gussie ventured, arching one brow. "It seems to me that Lord Trowbridge has been dangling after you rather much of late."

"Oh, no! Surely, ma'am, you are jesting. Why he is quite as old as my father! He has been no more than kind." Amanda had flushed to a deep red and tears glistened in her wide blue eyes.

"Well, well, as you say, my dear. Perhaps you had better hint him away, for if my perceptions are right he is about to single you out markedly. And he is a handsome man of considerable countenance and address, with several notable estates. Still, I can see the subject distresses you and I will say no more."

Mortified, Amanda cast about in her mind for some way to introduce a new topic. Augusta, thinking that the attentions of another gentleman to the girl *did* constitute a new topic, immediately plunged in again.

"Sir Harvey Moreton. Now there is a likely young man. A most fashionable pink-of-the-*ton* and of unimpeachable character!" Gussie glanced at Amanda. Though the girl dimpled at the mention of the personable Sir Harvey— whose shyness with the fair sex was renowned despite the many lures thrown out to so amiable and wealthy a catch— it was apparent even to Gussie's matchmaking eye that the subject was an embarrassment to her guest. "What do you think of making up a small party to go riding Tuesday next after the breakfast at Lady Singleham's? Or do you think a small dance party to instruct you young people in the newest steps?"

Amanda, knowing Lord Binghampton would join a riding party but shun a dancing party with equal force, indicated her preference for the first plan and Sara concurred.

That evening Augusta and Amanda were in a dither of excitement over the proposed entertainment, but Sara could not rouse much enthusiasm. Amanda wore a gown of palest peach satin with ecru French lace at the bodice and hem and a choker of amber beads on a matching ecru ribbon. Gussie had just received a new gown from Madame Olga which was of white silk with fine pin stripes of red and blue and had red-and-blue piping at the sleeves—all this in honor of her intended's country. Sara was undecided as to whether the sea-green embroidered silk or the light heather satin with white trimming would be more suitable. She was attempting to make up her mind when a very excited Amanda swirled into her room after the merest knock.

"Oh, do look, Sara! Aren't they lovely? Whatever shall I do?" she uttered breathlessly, proffering two waist corsages for inspection. One was a most unusual and quite expensive arrangement of dark blue and cream colored violets, tied with ribbons of peach, cream and pale green. The second was of dusty pink carnations with bright pink ribbons and obviously clashed discordantly with the peach fabric of Amanda's gown.

"Why, the violets, without a doubt!" Sara replied. "They will be perfect with your toilette."

"Perhaps I could wear the pink silk again," Amanda said.

A knowledgeable gleam came to Sara's eye. "May I ask who has sent you such lovely posies?" she inquired with a smile.

"Oh! The violets are from Sir Harvey Moreton, and the carnations from Lord Binghampton."

"Well, the carnations are very nice as far as they go, but certainly they are not as distinguished as the violets. I'm sure you will be the envy of your acquaintances when they see that someone has gone to a great deal of trouble to provide a corsage of flowers that are not only rare, but also out of season!"

"Yes," said Amanda much struck by this observation. "And they are *so* very beautiful. *Most* kind of Sir Harvey!"

"And," said Gussie, popping in the open door, "nothing pricks a young man's vanity more than seeing a young lady to whom he has shown *any* partiality wearing the flowers of a rival—and far more desirable flowers at that! I did not know young Moreton to possess such nice taste."

Amanda was swayed by the two older women's worldly wisdom almost as much as by the stunning effect of the cream and dark blue violets on her shimmering dress. She felt happy and quickly pinned the corsage in place.

Gussie was wearing a lovely arrangement of red and white rosebuds tied with blue ribbons and silver lace which Christopher had sent with a lovely note saying that "the wearer might inspire the buds to great beauty of bloom, but they could never match the fair rose who carried them." The American had also sent a posy of palest yellow flowers in gold lace for Sara to wear or carry, with his compliments, and a lace fan to Amanda.

Gussie and Amanda had sparkling eyes and rosy cheeks in anticipation of the evening's pleasures, but Sara's eyes had taken on a hard, bright glitter that made her aunt exclaim, "Sara, my love! Your eyes seem overbright and you have been becoming more flushed over the past few minutes. You are not taking a fever, are you?" She hurried to her niece and pressed a soft wrist to her forehead.

"I must admit I am not feeling quite the thing," Sara admitted. "I have been listless all day, but thought I was only a little tired."

"Oh, child! You are burning up! You must get into bed at once and have one of Dr. Porter's fever powders. I will send Witherall to Christopher with a note asking him to pick up Amanda and excuse us from the party." She turned to ring the bell, but Sara demurred.

"I think it is just a slight sniffle, and I will be fine with a little rest. I assure you I will sleep the whole evening so there is no use in your staying with me only to watch me snore!"

"Oh, she's becoming delirious," Augusta cried, "for Sara has never snored in her life!"

"No, no." Sara laughed. "I was just funning you. Really, I need a good sleep to shake this off. I have a little tickle in my throat and one of Witherall's good strong toddies will be all I need to put me right again. But I declare I will not rest well if I know you have missed such a treat because of me."

Gussie was not satisfied, but knowing her niece's determined will and that Sara would indeed only fret if she remained at home, Gussie decided to carry on with the evening's plans. "But we will come home early, poppet, to look in on you."

After much fussing the two ladies insisted on seeing Sara into bed and Augusta would not leave until Sara had swallowed one of the cachets that Dr. Porter had left when Gussie had been down with a fever the preceding winter. This was washed down with one of Witherall's special toddies, and in a short time Sara was pleasantly drowsy and relaxed. Amanda had bathed Sara's temples in lavender water and tucked her in with little motherly clucks, causing Sara to smile.

"Why Amanda, you are much at home at the bedside as in the ballroom!"

"Oh, yes," she acknowledged, "for my father has the gout and my mother is bronchial so that I have become quite experienced in the sickroom. And once"—she leaned forward and whispered conspiratorially—"I helped old Bob with a mare that was in foal. I was the only one that could calm poor dear Butterfly and the groom said she would have died without me there! Buy pray do not tell Mama, for she would be horrified."

Sara reassured her on this head and added that she would "promise not to be as troublesome as Butterfly so you may rest easy and enjoy the spectacle tonight."

As it appeared that the invalid was in no dire straits and would soon be asleep, Augusta and Amanda tiptoed out of the room and were ready when the Ames family arrived in their smart carriage. Soon they were on the way to Vauxhall to meet the rest of the party.

Mr. Ames had rented a booth that overlooked the lake

where the fireworks were to be shown and the ladies were enchanted with the view. They were joined by Lord Binghampton and Sir Harvey Moreton and a handsome and distinguished friend of Mr. Ames, Colonel Johnston of the Fourth Hussars. The Colonel expressed polite disappointment in Madame Sara Roche's absence, and also his profound delight in the beautiful and charming ladies who made up the party.

This last did not appear to please Binghampton, who took exception to the Colonel's marked attentions to Miss Bensome. And when he realized that she was wearing someone else's corsage, his usually even temper was a trifle strained. He turned to his compatriot, Sir Harvey, and muttered under his breath. "What airs that army fellow is giving himself, just because Miss Bensome is wearing his flowers. How was I to know my corsage would be such a poor color choice? Rather a show-off arrangement, eh?" Binghampton continued in disgruntled fashion.

"Didn't mean to show-off," Sir Harvey murmured self-deprecatingly.

"How do you know what the devil that rascal meant?" snapped Binghampton.

"Didn't send them!" his companion answered.

"What do you mean he didn't send them? Who else would have?" The young lord scowled.

"Happens I did," Sir Harvey said doggedly.

"*You!* I've never known you to dangle after any miss just out on the town," Binghampton said.

"Never met anyone as...as sweet—dash it!—as Miss Bensome," countered Sir Harvey. The two men glared in silence for a few seconds, but Augusta being a good hostess and not liking the Colonel's particular attentions to her young charge, soon included them in a lively discussion of a new book of poetry which was all the rage.

A repast of thinly shaved ham, cold lobster and sliced

beef was served with some elegant desserts and a good quantity of champagne for the older members of the party, and ratafia for Miss Bensome.

"But you must try a little champagne, my dear," encouraged the Colonel. "Champagne and fireworks go together like moonlight and lovers."

This remark was overheard only by Lord Binghampton who was prepared to leap across the table and take Johnston by the throat. Amanda's blue eyes widened in alarm and caused a flood of protectiveness to flow over Binghampton, almost overwhelming him. He managed to keep his head, and entering the conversation, returned the talk to a general discussion. Eventually, he maneuvered so that he escorted Amanda on a stroll through the walks with Gussie and Mr. Ames.

When Amanda turned as if to invite the Colonel and Sir Harvey to join them, Binghampton unthinkingly gave her a nip on the arm as he would have done to silence his sister. Coming from a large family, she automatically responded by closing her lips until they were strolling down a pleasant path lit by multicolored lanterns.

"Why did you pinch me?" she asked ingenuously. "Was I about to say something I should not?"

"I didn't pinch you . . . oh, er . . . good Lord, so I did! Beg your pardon." He attempted to recover himself. "It's simply that army fellow has been monopolizing you all evening. I wanted you to myself for a little while, if you don't mind too much."

Amanda was so pleased with this little speech that she didn't stop to ponder the impropriety of a young man of fashion pinching a young lady of quality to gain her attention, and the two ambled down the walkways in front of their chaperones in amiable conversation.

"About the flowers," Binghampton began. Amanda

flushed crimson, and would have innocently apologized for not wearing them if he had not gone on.

"It was very clumsy of me not to inquire as to your gown. Usually you wear pink or white and I thought my flowers would suit."

"Oh, so thoughtful! They were lovely; it quite broke my heart not to be able to carry them tonight," Amanda responded artlessly. "I almost changed my toilette but . . ." She stopped, aghast.

"By Jove, did you? What a capital girl you are, Miss Bensome! It is comfortable to talk with a female who is so frank-hearted, and not all coy simpers!" Here, the older couple caught up with them and no further confidences were exchanged, but Binghampton perhaps held Miss Bensome's arm a little closer as they returned to their booth, and he stayed glued to her side through the exhibit of fireworks.

"Oh, did you ever see anything so beautiful?" Augusta asked as a rocket burst in green, gold and blue blossoms against the black velvet sky.

"Yes, I most certainly did!" Christopher smiled down at her with a flash of white teeth in the darkness. The Colonel had gone to visit friends in the next booth leaving the two young men to vie for Amanda's favors. A shrieking catherine wheel of scarlet and gold arced across the sky followed by simultaneous bombs of green and white, causing Miss Bensome to utter a startled little squeak.

"Frightened?" Sir Harvey asked, patting her small hand.

"No," Amanda replied. "They are just so very, very incredible."

Never one to pass up an advantage, Binghampton spoke up. "We're having fireworks and a dance at Kennerly Court just after the Season for my mother's birthday. If you think you would like to come, I will have my mother send invitations to Green Dolphin Street."

Miss Bensome did not know how to reply to this, for an invitation to the country by a young man was not casually offered unless there was some sort of understanding. Fortunately, Binghampton was oblivious to this line of thought at the time, and as they were joined again by Colonel Johnston, it was not necessary for Amanda to reply.

With a fiery tableau outlining the Colosseum in Rome, the leaning tower of the city of Pisa and the noble columns of the Parthenon, the fireworks display concluded, receiving wild applause and cheers and whistles from the spectators.

CHAPTER TEN

Across town, the Earl of Ramsey basked also in a cozy atmosphere, in the library of his town house in St. James Square. He sat in contented silence sipping a glass of port. His long, elegant legs stretched out before him, he contemplated the ruby color of the wine flashing in the cutglass goblet as the candles flickered in the breeze from the open windows. He had bowed out of Princess Metzenberger's drum as early as civility permitted, for he had found the evening curiously dull, the company insipid. At last he had slipped away after making his excuses to his hostess and joined a few close friends at Waitier's where a good deal of champagne had been downed in an unusually short amount of time.

Captain Syminton, a tried-and-true friend, had begun

the evening by ribbing his friend since childhood about the status of his marriage plans.

"Well, Edward! If anyone had told me during the campaign that you would turn into such a slow-top once you shed your regimentals, I would have called him a liar to his face. For all it's not been formally announced in the *Gazette*, the whole town knows you're pledged to be shackled to the Kennerly girl. And a prime 'un she is, by Jove!"

The Earl looked over his glass pointedly at his companion but vouchsafed no reply.

"You've never been behindhand with the ladies, my friend," the Captain continued with a lazy drawl. "Could it be you've lost your touch since you came so unexpectedly to your honors? When you was plain Major 'Wild Ned' Stanhope and you set your sights on something there was nothing short of death and the devil would keep you at bay!"

"Why I didn't let you drown in that river when I had the chance, I'll never know—nor cease to regret!" The Earl sighed, a small smile belying his words.

"Pah! Don't pretend it was to save my life you jumped into the raging brew. You just wanted to see if you could swim it, and used my mischance for an excuse. Not that you ever needed an excuse to do something dangerous and foolhardy with that reckless Ramsey blood in your veins!" the officer snorted.

"Well, just remember that it is that wild Ramsey blood that . . . er, brought me to my honors. If my cousin hadn't come a cropper racing his curricle down Stepley Hill, I would still be in the regiment and have to put up with your conversation on a regular basis rather than once in a while!" Ramsey laughed, clapping his friend affectionately on the back.

They lit up some fine black *cigarillos* and puffed a cloud in companionable silence for a bit. Soon they were joined by Lord Hepstill and his cousin Mr. Tinsdale and after exchanging a few pleasantries the four settled down to a fast-paced game of cards. Ramsey had all the luck and the pile of counters in front of his place grew steadily higher till Hepstill protested.

"I say, it's supposed to be 'lucky at love, unlucky at cards,' and you seem to be doing just the opposite."

"Oh, 'Wild Ned' was never one to stand by the conventions, you know," announced the Captain, drawing a laugh from the other two men but not before he noticed the strange look that flickered briefly over the Earl's handsome face and the bright amber glint his eyes took on before he carefully schooled his features.

"Speaking of Luck," Captain Syminton smoothly addressed Mr. Tinsdale, "I hear you snapped up Finchley's bays the moment he even *thought* of parting with them. They look to be sweet steppers!"

Mr. Tinsdale beamed and recounted his coup over the other admirers of the matched bays formerly belonging to said Mr. Finchley, and the talk went along these lines until the party broke up well after midnight. The Captain walked Ramsey to his town house but declined an invitation to come in for port. As he took his leave the dragoon officer turned suddenly to his friend.

"Know it's not my business, Ned, but are you having trouble in bringing your fiancée up to point? If so," he continued since Edward made no move to stop him, "I can only think you've no heart for the matter, for the woman you can't bring round has not been born!"

Edward looked at his shirt cuff and carelessly flicked away an imaginary speck of lint before answering.

"You are too shrewd as ever, Jack. The thing is I'm committed and there is nothing more to be said."

"What? Resignation to fate? You must be queer in the attic if you're in a scrape and feel your hands tied! Pah, but civilian life has made you a regular sapskull, for the Ned I knew could always find a dozen ways out of an inescapable position. Why the Portuguese used to call you 'The Ghost' for the way you would slip out every time they thought they had you!"

"An engagement to an eligible young lady of fashion can hardly be compared to a military campaign!" Ramsey laughed in spite of himself.

"So you say, but I've escaped a few clutches myself and I *know* you're wrong!" The Captain joined in the laughter. "Still, whatever made you offer for the girl if your heart didn't go with your hand?"

"It was high time I was married and got an heir to the estate. If I should cock up my toes the title passes to my nephew Jaspar, and a damned loose fish that one is! The least I could do for my late cousin is safely secure the estates he made his life's work by providing myself with a full nursery. Damn, man, don't look at me like that! Lady Pamela would shed no tears for me if I stuck my spoon in the wall this night. She would only mourn my fortune and the fact that she had not been made countess before my demise."

The Captain uttered a low whistle and looked at his friend with a subdued glance. "It seems there would be no love lost at all if this whole affair should collapse. Would you be in a happier frame if there were some way to break off the engagement?"

"Good God, man! I can't cry off; and even if I were so ramshackle a fellow it would be a shabby thing to do when, as you have told me, all of London knows of our betrothal!" the Earl exclaimed.

"Well, I won't beg your pardon because that's not at all what I meant. What I had in mind was to ascertain your feelings if the lady in question should cry off." Symington eyed his companion speculatively.

"It sounds as if there's more to this than you have said," Edward questioned, lifting one slanting eyebrow. "Speak your piece!"

"There seems to be another fellow who has caught your intended's eye, from the *on-dits* circulating. And today I saw the fair Pamela making rather a fool of herself over some fellow in the Park. You'll pardon my bluntness, but we've been in many a close scrape together, and you've set me on the right track with a flea in my ear more times than I can count!"

"You're a good fellow," Ramsey responded placing his hand on his friend's arm, "and closer to me than any brother could have been. But tell me, who is this interloper?"

"That I didn't discover, for the officer with me didn't know him either."

"Was he quite tall, blond hair with some gray at the sides?"

His friend nodded assent, not understanding the strange light shining in the Earl's eyes. "I did hear a companion call him 'Christopher,'" the officer added as his memory was jogged.

"Famous! By all that's holy, I may come about yet!" Ramsey cried in delight. Bidding his friend a hasty good night, he went up the stairs and disappeared, leaving a very bewildered captain staring up at the closed door.

Inside, Ramsey discarded his hat and walking stick on a small inlaid table in the hallway and waited for Jarvis to remove his coat.

"I thought I gave you distinct orders not to wait up for me."

"Yes, milord, however, as I wasn't sleepy I thought I'd sit up a while longer." Since the butler's heavy eyes gave the lie to his glib statement, Edward only gave an affectionate snort. Jarvis had known "Master Ned" in short coats at Ramsey Park where he'd run wild in the summers by the late Earl's indulgence. Jarvis was glad he had waited up for his master, for he noted with some slight trepidation the dangerous sparkle in the Earl's eye which usually denoted some deviltry afoot.

"Well, off with you!" Edward said when he was divested of his topcoat. "I'll sit in the library over some of that excellent port for a while before turning in."

Jarvis had no choice, but as he went through the baize door to the servants quarters he felt a qualm. "Not in his cups, he isn't, but I'd rather see him a trifle bosky than with that restless air about him!" Jarvis, having known three generations of Ramseys, went to sleep with what he told himself was "a feeling in the bones!"

Too restless to sit and too wakeful to sleep, the Earl decided the night was young and fine for a walk. He picked up his hat and walking stick and let himself out into the cool air, paying no heed to the ominous clouds scudding in from the west on the heels of a freshening wind. After walking for some time he looked about at his surroundings and discovered that his feet had carried him, all unknowing, to Green Dolphin Street. He was surprised, for he had started out in quite another direction entirely. Well, he'd light up a *cigarillo* and blow a cloud before starting back to his town house.

Sara had slept for a few hours and then awakened with a very heavy head. The hot toddy had aided the effects of the fever powder, leaving her with the strangest feeling that her mind was floating outside her body. While her fever had not risen alarmingly, it remained elevated just enough to make her disoriented and restless. It was stuffy in her bedroom, for Amanda had closed the windows to prevent a draft.

Opening the casement, she leaned over the sill for a breath of air. The night was warm, but not uncomfortably so, for a cool breeze had sprung up, promising rain before long. The cool air felt so good that Sara thought she would go down to the garden and sit for a while. Witherall had gone to the pub to have a few pints with the coachman across the road, and as no one was home but the little parlor maid, sound asleep on the upper floor, Sara decided to do no more than throw a dressing gown of gauzy lawn over her filmy nightshift.

On the stairway she had to pause and grasp the rail, her head spinning. She descended more carefully and made her way across the foyer to the studio. Walking past the easel where the Earl of Ramsey's portrait waited, she went to the painting of Janie Ames. The face and figure were almost the way she had seen them in her mind's eye, but the background was too trite, too forced.

Sara sat in a small side chair and gazed at the portrait, but no inspiration came. The painting was placed on an easel in front of the tall windows leading out to the gardens. She went to the windows and pulled back the heavy drapes, the exertion and slight fever making the thin gown and robe cling to her damp skin. Smelling of welcome rain to come, the breeze danced through the french window, rustling even the curtains on the far side of the room.

Sara sat down again and gratefully felt light wind blow across her face, cooling her flushed cheeks. As she sat staring at Janie's portrait, an idea struck her. The painting of the girl was framed by the opened windows and their green draperies and Sara knew she must change the background to a sophisticated drawing room with tall open windows, just as she saw before her now. She would keep the deer kneeling peacefully at Janie's feet, but what could she use to pull the symbolism of the painting together in a harmonious whole?

Through the open windows a bank of clouds moved on the wind, revealing a sky of deep startling blue sparkled with hundreds of brilliant stars scintillating across its breadth. An inspiration came to Sara; she would paint, high in the sky seen above the girl's head, the Pleiades, as a shining coronet, crowning Miss Ames's unaffected beauty and naturalness.

She stood up, her thought clearer but her head beginning to ache abominably, and searched among her utensils and tubes for the right colors and materials. She found the strong, handsome face of the Earl of Ramsey intruding itself until it completely overwhelmed the picture of Janie Ames she had been trying to concentrate her thoughts on. Against her will she was transported back to the night of the Gravestons' ball, the night he had led her into the garden, where among the scented roses, he had tried to make love to her. She remembered the feel of his strong arms around her, the warmth of his lips on hers. Sara raised a hand to her lips and touched them softly, seeing again the look in his eyes as he pulled her close.

Her mind had been spinning with so many thoughts and sensations. The feeling of safety, of having reached a safe harbor. Suspicion and confusion, wondering why he was making her the object of his attentions. The sudden pang of desire that seemed to rise from the pit of her stomach, spreading upward to her breasts and throat, spreading down into her loins until she had pressed her body against his in the ancient response of female to male.

Even now, thinking of it brought heat to her body. What must he think of her? Did he think she would be susceptible to dalliance, perhaps an affair with him out of the needs of her body? Or had he heard the vicious whispers of gossip that had followed her when Jerome had fought and died in that stupid, useless duel?

Could she blame Ramsey for thinking of her as he must,

especially after she had responded to his experienced love-making. Even Jerome had been embarrassed by her sensual nature. Once, shocked, he had called her a Jezebel. How strange, Sara thought, that men would look down on women for the very things they encouraged them to feel and do.

A small, soft sound drifted in through the open window. She had thought Muse was inside, but decided the kitten must have slipped into the studio and out the door when her back was turned.

Out beyond the wall that separated the garden from the side street, the Earl of Ramsey quietly reconnoitered. He had seen the dim light flickering erratically through the iron grill set in the brick wall and realized it came from the studio. He knew no one was allowed in there in Sara's absence and as he knew the ladies of the house were at Vauxhall Gardens, decided to investigate. With a lithe movement he was over the wall and dropping down into the garden. His hand brushed some loose mortar from the wall as he leaped on to it.

Sara, hearing the sound, smiled to herself. Her first thought was that it was the intrepid American, coming to court his beautiful and romantic fiancée. He had smiled a hint about a moonlight serenade, and as the moon was now a shining silver disc half-hidden by the billowing clouds, Sara wondered if Christopher had come to woo Gussie. Strange that she hadn't heard Gussie and Amanda return from their outing, but perhaps the effects of the toddy and fever cachet had still been strong. Even now, although her head seemed clear, she was aware of a feeling of removal from her senses, as if she were looking at the world through a pane of thick glass. But while aware of this sensory distortion, she was oblivious to a lack of logical progression in her thoughts as well as to her lack of appropriate apparel.

Sara stepped into the doorway and looked about. "Muse?" she called softly, but the rising wind snatched the words from her lips making them indistinguishable to the Earl. She went forward, lifting the candle. "Who's there?" she called softly.

Ramsey, who had just dropped over the wall, making the noise that had alerted Sara, suddenly stopped short in alarm. It was no prowler, after all, and his action seemed a bit rash in view of the facts. He was very aware that skulking in a lady's garden in the dead of night was not precisely the way to endear oneself to that lady! Damn the family inheritance of impetuosity which was both the boon and the bane of the Ramsey name! One of Edward's fellow officers had remarked that the Ramsey family motto should be changed from "Action Now" to "Act First, Think Later." The Earl drew himself up in such a way that he blended into the dappled shadows as he'd learned to do in the Peninsular campaign. He held very still.

Sara went down the three steps from the studio to the garden, but the little walled area seemed serene and empty, only the branches of the espaliered pear tree seeming to sway with the stirring wind. Even with the imminent rain, the night was fine with the strange expectancy that fills the air at such a time. She lifted her face to the breeze, feeling the kiss of the wind on her skin as it lifted, then molded her gossamer light gown and robe to her body. Her candle winked out. She stood there, drinking in the cool wine of the night, still feeling rather disembodied, although her mind was clear. She reached back and undid the ribbon that held her hair captive in a single thick braid, loosening it to stream over her shoulders like a shining sable cloak.

Concealed in the darkness, Ramsey caught his breath at the sight of Sara's beauty. Her innocence of his presence and her vulnerability made him more acutely aware of his trespassing and he was so angry with his own fecklessness that he clenched his fists. At that moment he wanted nothing more than to have Sara turn and go back to the house so he could escape from a very awkward situation before he was discovered, causing severe embarrassment to both. He held himself immobile hoping she would go in to escape the quickening breeze.

Sara, while thrilling to the primordial feeling the brisk breeze and beginning flickers of lightning had evoked, was becoming aware also of the sharp drop in temperature. Turning, she was about to go back to the studio, when there was a loud squeal followed by a sharp hiss and a very loud crashing thud over by the pear tree. Muse streaked past her like a small bolt of lightning and disappeared into the house.

Ramsey, relieved at his chance to escape, had begun to move to his right for good leverage to pull himself over the wall. His boot came down, not on the soft earth of the garden, but on something far softer that had shot out from under his foot and thrown him off balance.

He was unable to catch himself and fell heavily, stunned. He shut his eyes involuntarily for a few seconds while colored rockets burst and flared in his brain.

When he opened them, Sara was coming hesitantly across the flagstones toward him, just as an enormous crack of thunder sounded and icy rain poured out of the shattered clouds. He rose to his hands and knees and shook his head sharply. If he had frightened her with a kiss at the ball, finding him hiding in her garden at this time of night would surely have a devastating effect!

Making her way across the garden in the blowing wind and rain, her thin nightclothes molded to her skin so that she might as well have been naked, Sara came closer. His discovery was inevitable. Edward, fighting to control the sudden wave of desire that possessed him, took a sharp intake of breath that was audible even over the wind and rain.

Sara heard the sound and stepped closer. "Christopher? Is that you? I can't see a thing—are you all right?"

"Christopher, is it, by God!" Ramsey roared, springing to his feet. He took in her hair and gown plastered to her body and felt such a rage of jealousy as he had never thought to know. Before Sara could move, he had grasped her shoulders roughly and drawn her tightly to him.

"Christopher, is it!" Edward repeated savagely. "By God, I'll make you forget you ever set eyes on him!" He kissed her hungrily, ruthlessly, as she trembled in his arms. At last he drew his lips away from hers, though never slackening his grasp.

"Does your Christopher kiss you like this? Does he make you tremble like this?"

"Let me go!" she cried, struggling futilely against his superior strength.

"No! I will *not* let you go! You run from my kisses but run to his arms like a wanton!" He kissed her again with passionate intensity and Sara responded, pressing her body against his, answering his kisses with her own. Her arms twined around his neck and she was oblivious to the chill rain falling as she felt the warmth of his strong hands caressing, molding her body to his.

Then with a shock she recalled herself and attempted to push away from his chest where he held her so tightly. She was afraid, not of him but of her own passions. "Please! Let me go," she whispered, her eyes like sapphires in the moonlight.

Edward smiled sardonically. "Is that what you want? I think not!" He bent his head again and kissed her while he held her close in the crook of his left arm and his right hand reached up and began to expertly undo the little fastenings at the top of her gown. He kept his lips pressed on hers while his hand slid inside the bodice of her nightgown and cupped the round breast in his hand, stroking the nipple with his thumb.

A sound, half sigh, half moan, escaped Sara when he lifted his head; he stood looking down on her with a victor's look of triumph illuminating his face.

"I think," he said hoarsely, "that you want me as much as I want you!" He pulled her so close that she could hardly breathe. "Do you? Tell me, Sara!" he demanded fiercely. "Say you want me as I want you!"

"Yes, oh, yes!" she answered, reaching up to pull his head down to hers. The garden seemed to start spinning around her and she swayed a fraction. The Earl stooped as if to sweep her up into his arms and carry her into the house but the sound of a frantic voice called out.

"Sara! Sara are you out there? Oh, dear! I should have never gone and left her alone when she was ill!" Augusta's rich voice floated out above the sounds of diminishing rain.

Sara pulled herself out of Edward's embrace, aghast. He stood as if turned to stone, then quickly peeled off his coat and threw it over her shoulders, hiding her near nakedness. He stared numbly at her. She looked as if she were in a trance. Like a sleepwalker, she turned slowly, went down the path and then up the three steps into the house.

One look at her niece's white face and glazed eyes was enough for Gussie. She bundled Sara quickly up the stairs and into her room before Amanda or anyone else could see her. Gussie didn't ask how she came to be out in the garden in a storm and draped in the exquisitely tailored coat of a gentleman. Instead, she got her into dry clothes and tucked her into the high bed with its rose-covered hangings and pillows. Then she pulled the bell cord violently before going to the fireplace and stirring the indifferent flames to vigorous life.

CHAPTER ELEVEN

"Witherall, go at once and fetch Dr. Porter. Tell him to lose no time! You, girl," Augusta directed the maid, "put some water on to boil immediately. I will want plenty of strong hot tea. And heat up the chicken broth. Oh dear, oh dear!" she muttered. Witherall, stony-faced, was off as soon as the horse was saddled, and the maid flew down to the kitchen, her eyes streaming. It was as much the vision of the competent Gussie in near hysterics as the pale unmoving face of Sara lying so still beneath the comforters that unnerved the servants, and they followed their instructions with heavy hearts.

When Witherall returned with the news that the doctor was on his way, Gussie sent him out once more, this time with a hastily scribbled note for Christopher Ames. Then she sat on the side of the bed and sponged Sara's fevered brow with lavender water, uttering little distressed sounds. She'd had neither chick nor child and the white little face on the pillow before her was dearer to her than anyone could possibly know.

After an agonizing interval a sound of an approaching carriage came closer through the silent streets and in a few minutes Dr. Porter was ushered into the sickroom.

"My dear Mrs. Roche! What is to do here? I've never known the dear little lady to be ill before." He hurried over, picked up Sara's limp wrist, felt the tumultuous pulse. Her breathing was fairly rapid, and the doctor became grave as he catalogued the implications of these signs. He reached out and lifted Sara's eyelids, giving a quiet sigh of relief as the lids resisted his fingers before opening. She mumbled something indistinct and attempted to turn her head away from the bright lamplight.

"Well that's a good sign," the doctor murmured. "How long has she been like this?" he asked Augusta.

"Just before we went out this evening she complained of feeling out of sorts but she insisted we not alter our plans," she replied, unable to keep the anguish out of her voice. "When we returned I went to look in on her and she was gone! I found her out in the garden in the pouring rain, walking strangely as if she were in a daze. I helped her upstairs and into some dry nightclothes and she has been lying here like this ever since."

"Did she say anything to you?" Dr. Porter asked.

"No, not a word," Gussie wrung her hands while the doctor continued his examination. "Oh, it is all my fault! How could I have gone out and left her?"

"Nonsense!" the physician snapped. "I have known you for too long to think that you would have left her here alone if she showed even the slightest sign of an inflammation; and since she has always been sound as a bell there was no reason to guess she'd come to this pass. Besides, she didn't contract this just now in the rain, although only time will tell if it caused her any harm."

"You must tell me..." Gussie began, but the doctor had spent so many hours at the bedside that he knew what her words would be.

"I can't say yet what course the illness will take, but Sara is well-nourished and healthy and should pull through with good nursing. There's a lot of this popping up in town the past few days—a common childhood complaint, but one that comes out queerly in adults if they should come down with it. I'll be calling round again about ten of the morning. Make sure you send me word if things go worse with her."

Shortly after the doctor left, Mr. Ames was shown into the drawing room where he waited anxiously until Gussie entered. He strode forward, catching her hands in his large ones before pulling her into his arms. Gussie wept a bit, apologized for being a watering pot and then poured out her self-condemnations and fears. The American, being a man of experience, soothed her in the best way possible.

"Oh, Christopher! What would I do without you!" she said when he at last released her from his embrace.

"*That* is something I will make sure you never have to find out!" he vowed, drying her tears with his linen handkerchief. He left shortly after, begging Gussie to send for him if there was any problem and promising to return in the morning.

Sara lay as still as when Gussie had left. She watched Amanda tenderly applying balm to Sara's lips, already dry from the rising fever.

"Go to bed, child," Augusta said. "I will sit with her till morning."

"No," said Amanda firmly. "Tomorrow you will be deluged with inquiries as to her health and you will have your hands full canceling our engagements as well as running the household. Please let me do this for you. I am wide awake and feel fresh now while you are looking sadly pulled!" The young woman went over to Gussie and placed her hand gently on her sleeve. "Go to bed, and you can take a watch in the morning. I will call you if there is the slightest change."

Amanda was right, Gussie acknowledged, and if she let herself become too out of frame, she could be of no help to Sara at all. So at last she lay down atop the cover— she had not thought to sleep, but in a short time was deep in uneasy slumber.

Unaware of the trouble in Green Dolphin Street, Ramsey had gone back to his house in a fearsome temper. He stalked into the library, loosened his neckcloth and sat down with a full brandy decanter which he proceeded to empty. By the time the servants were stirring he was, as Jarvis put it, more than a trifle disguised. Therefore, it was with some trepidation but no very real surprise that Jarvis heard his master tell Hinckle, his valet, to pack a small bag. The Earl only said he would be gone a few days and to have his secretary make whatever excuses he deemed necessary. Refusing to take Hinckle along, Edward called for his curricle and he was off on the northern road before the sun had done more than peek over the horizon.

He had no destination in mind, only wanting to put a great distance between himself and London. He proceeded to do so at a clipping pace. He sprung the bays when he reached the highway and kept up such a breakneck speed it required all his skill and concentration to stay on the road. As this manner of driving gave him no time for any other thought it suited his needs well.

As the Earl drove out with the rising sun, Gussie went to check on Sara. Amanda greeted her quietly and assured her there had been no change for the worse. Sara still lay unmoving except for the rapid rise and fall of her chest with every shallow breath.

Not knowing of Sara's illness, Lord Binghampton came to make a morning call and pay his respects after the evening's festivities. He was quite disappointed to be informed that Mrs. Roche and Miss Bensome were not at home to callers. Since he had never been refused entry before, and Witherall's demeanor was cool, almost harsh, Bing could only think he had offended in some way. When Mr. Ames pulled up and was allowed in almost immediately, the young lord could only surmise that his transgression was a most serious one. He left, casting about in his mind for any incident of the previous night that might shed light on the matter.

By nightfall Binghampton, still puzzled as to what it might be, arrived at his parents' town house to find his sister causing an uproar.

If it was not the outside of enough that Ramsey had failed to show to go riding in the Row, it was certainly more than could be tolerated to have him fail to show up for their evening at the opera. It was only because the dinner party for once consisted solely of the immediate family that Lady Pamela was saved from complete mortification.

Neither her mother's pleadings nor her brother's threat to box her ears quieted the young lady as she castigated her fiancé for all to hear. At last Binghampton took her by the shoulders and shook her soundly.

"If you forget what is due your consequence, *I* do not!

And I refuse to have my sister screeching like a fishwife for all the servants to hear. Now stop, or I *will* box your ears!" This violence from her easygoing brother silenced Lady Pamela abruptly. She had no doubt he would make good his threat.

"Now go to your room until you are ready to conduct yourself properly!" Binghampton adjured as he went into the yellow salon, leaving his astonished mother to look after his departing back.

"Now, what has got into *him*?" that beleaguered lady said wonderingly. Lady Pamela gathered her dignity and went up to her room, not to meditate on her deportment, or lack thereof; instead she wrote a short and succinct note to Ramsey. Then she went downstairs to the library and spent some time examining the outlines of the North American continent with a small, satisfied smile.

Back in Green Dolphin Street, things remained less satisfactory; Dr. Porter had arrived to find his patient had suddenly become restless and instead of lying quietly was now tossing and turning agitatedly. Her breathing was fast and harsh, and occasionally she would mumble something aloud that her attendants were unable to comprehend.

"Do you think she is going into a crisis?" Gussie worriedly asked.

"Not in the graver meaning of the word. I think rather that she is beginning to throw off the inflammation and once the fever breaks she soon will be back in tune. I will leave you some powders to give her when she is more alert," he said rummaging in his leather bag. He gave the packets to Amanda with instructions for their use. "Should she come to her senses tonight, try to get some heartening broth into her and perhaps a little calf-foot jelly. I'll be round again in the morning."

The doctor's diagnosis was correct, and by morning

Sara, though wan and weak, was once more in full possession of her faculties. Dr. Porter arrived and promised to stay long enough for a relieved but very tired Amanda to go to her room for a nap, and when Mr. Ames came by, Augusta was able to take a stroll outdoors on his arm.

Thus it happened that Lord Binghampton, once more calling in Green Dolphin Street, was again told that the ladies of the household were not at home to visitors. He proffered a bouquet of flowers for Miss Bensome which was accepted by a reserved Witherall without ceremony and once more was left standing in the street. Pamela having fits, Ramsey disappearing without a word and now being snubbed by Miss Bensome and her sponsors! Had all of London slipped its moorings? Bitterly, Bing went in search of some cheering company.

By evening, after looking in at White's, putting on the gloves at Jackson's parlor for a few rounds and then going on to a dinner party at Sir Harvey Moreton's digs, Binghampton decided that the Season was becoming a dead bore with time on his hands. There was really nowhere at all to go, unless one counted the opera or the music hall or Almack's or indeed anything else that came to mind. He heaved a heavy sigh.

"Never seen you so blue-deviled, Bing! Woman trouble?" Moreton asked hopefully.

"Oh, just a bit knocked-up by all the festivities," Binghampton replied with a languid gesture. "I might get away for a few days."

"P'raps a sojourn in the country would do you a bit of good!" his friend agreed, being strongly of the school of thought that all is indeed fair in love and war.

"Yes. Cranshaw invited me to his place near Pickstowe. He had to go up on some business affair. By Jove, I'll do just that!" As good as his word, Binghampton was off early the next morning to join Mr. George Cranshaw for a few weeks rustication.

All that week the weather remained warm but dry. By Friday Sara was able to come downstairs for the first time since her illness, though only to the floor where the drawing room waited in its serene beauty and not down to her studio. When Dr. Porter came to see how the invalid was doing, she felt so much stronger that she begged him to let her go out for a drive on the morrow if the clear weather held.

"I see no objection since you are getting on so well. As a matter of fact some fresh air will help put the roses back in your cheeks!"

"Oh, that sounds so lovely!" Sara exclaimed. "Ah, if I were only in the country eating fresh eggs and ham, I declare I would be fit as a fiddle in no time."

"Well, why don't you go then!" the physician answered. "I think by the first of the week, or at the latest, Wednesday, you should be able to undertake a short journey, if it is broken with rest stops."

"But it is the middle of the Season! We couldn't leave now. No. No. I will do very well here for a few more weeks."

"Nonsense!" asserted Gussie, coming into the room during the last exchange. "I am feeling quite worn to the bone with all the balls and picnics and whatnot. As for Amanda, she is pale. You must know that she is used to walking and riding every day near her home, and I am totally convinced that nothing would suit us all as much as the quieter pace the country life offers."

Since Amanda came in with Sara's cordial at this time and she was in truth very pale and rather downcast, Sara fell in with Gussie's plans and placed everything in her aunt's capable hands.

Still, it was Wednesday before Dr. Porter officially gave his patient leave to travel, waiting until Sara was feeling very well for three days, saying that she would thank him in the end! And by the time they arrived at the property they had rented near the village of Pickstowe, Sara was indeed grateful to him. They had made the journey in three stages, in Mr. Ames's comfortable traveling coach, stopping for luncheon at a posting house where he had bespoken private rooms so that Sara could lie down and rest for an hour afterward. Later on, they had a light supper at a country inn and the sliced roast beef and veal pie with asparagus did much to revive the entire party. Refreshed, they resumed their travels and shortly before eight o'clock they turned into the road that led to their final destination. Mr. Ames declined to come in for refreshment and rode back to the Boar's Head Inn where his valet and luggage awaited him.

A high stone wall with iron gates led down a winding drive to a pleasant red-brick, half-timbered house. The rosy light of early evening glimmered on the open casement windows. As they approached the house, a break in the stand of tall willow trees edging the road gave a vista of sparkling water, and they soon passed a small lake with ducks and geese moving calmly on the shining surface. The front walk was charming with larkspurs, phlox and carnations in gay profusion and the inside of the house was as cozy and welcoming as the exterior. The greetings of the housekeeper, Mrs. Moll, and the cook, Mrs. Flynn, left nothing to be desired. Polly, the ruddy-faced housemaid arrived in the long drawing room with the very welcome tea tray to the travelers' delight.

Witherall and Augusta tried to convince Sara to go to her room and retire early after the rigors of the journey.

She was so heartened and intrigued by her new surroundings, however, that a cup of hot tea with toast was all she
needed to restore her flagging energies. Gussie, having
worried about Sara and Amanda all through the journey,
found herself a trifle out of frame and insisted a little over
an hour later that they retire, the better to explore when
they were fresh in the morning.

Sara was alone—alone with her thoughts—for the first
time since she had become ill. Amanda or Gussie had been
there when she went to sleep and again when she woke
up from her disordered dreams.

All through the early days of her convalescence, she
had been troubled by vague dreams of Janie Ames and
Lord Ramsey and falling stars—falling, falling all around
her. What was dream and what memory was difficult to
decipher in her fevered state. Now, although the recollec-
tion was faulty, she was certain of two things. Ramsey
had for some unimaginable reason been in her garden; the
proof of his coat with his own elusive scent could not be
denied. And she had thrown herself into his arms, returning
his passion with her own, admitting her need for him. That
she recalled with awful clarity.

She realized that she must have wandered down the
stairs and into her studio in her night gown. What had
possessed her to go out into the garden in such a state of
undress in the cold rain, and what the Earl was doing there
she had no idea at all. She tried to push away the memory of Ramsey's strong arms about her, his eyes alight
with a raging fire as he looked down at her. His face was
burned into her mind like an after image from staring at
the sun.

Next morning Gussie and Amanda went out to explore
the grounds while Sara slept. They found a pleasant old-
fashioned garden with pink delphinium and marigolds.
Paths of smooth gravel and brick led down to the small

lake. Here they sat on the stone bench and watched the ducks fighting over crusts of bread the kitchen maid had thrown out earlier, while the majestic goose and gander ignored them as if the whole squabble were beneath their dignity. Amanda and Gussie were not fooled, having seen the geese greedily pushing the ducks aside until they were glutted.

"This is almost perfect, is it not?"

"And what would make it completely perfect?" Gussie asked very offhandedly, her eyes shrewdly watching her young charge.

"Oh . . . nothing, really, Just an expression, you know," Amanda said, eyes downcast. "Oh, look at the butterfly on the lawn!"

Gussie recognized an evasive maneuver and sighed. How could she be a good matchmaker if no one confided in her? Well, she would still do her best. After all she did have two eyes in her head!

A soft step on the gravel path drew their attention. Sara came along the path from the house. While her eyes were shadowed and her cheeks pale, her step seemed sprightlier than before they had arrived, and as she went on to explain, her appetite was back to normal, ". . . for I've just polished off a plate of fried eggs, ham and sliced potatoes! No more invalid food for me!"

"That's good news, indeed!" Her aunt beamed. "We'll have you plump as a partridge in a few weeks with this clear air and wholesome food."

They basked in the warm sunshine and chatted until Augusta said the light was becoming so strong that she would fetch their hats to protect their complexions. She was on her way back to the house when the sound of horses hooves coming up the long drive heralded the arrival of Christopher Ames.

He hailed his fiancée and pulled up alongside her as

she reached the side drive. A skillful movement and he was off the carriage to plant a hearty kiss on her cheek, his free hand encircling her waist. With her gold head bent toward his shoulder the two lovers disappeared past the laurel trees on the way to the stableyard.

Sara and Amanda looked at each other and smiled. "It is so sweet to see their affection, is it not?" Sara said.

"Yes," Amanda replied absently with a small exhalation of breath. "It is good to know that love may work out happily for some people."

Sara reached out and took the girl's hand in hers. "You have not confided in me and I have no wish to intrude myself, but I am aware that you have been unhappy for some time."

Amanda looked down for a moment, biting her lip. Then she looked up at Sara, blinking away the tears that filled her blue eyes.

"It doesn't signify. I have been foolish, seeing attentions and interest where none was intended. I suppose it comes from being country-bred. The... young men of my acquaintance... well, they did not offer compliments unless they were meant. And if any gentleman paid any sort of particular attentions to a young lady, everyone knew what that signified. I have erred in taking London ways too seriously, and for that no one is at fault but myself. Do not worry," she continued, sitting up a little straighter with her head held high. "I shall soon come about with no harm done except to my pride!" She smiled a rather watery smile.

Sara was not fooled by her words and noted with an ache the way Amanda's lips quivered. "I must say something to you that you may think is none of my affair and the words may sound unfeeling and hard, but say it I must. When love is disappointed, we feel we can never, ever love again. We feel we are done with trust and caring and being open to wounds. Well, it is painful, but in time the pain goes away. The pain becomes a memory of pain." She searched the girl's face earnestly. "It takes time, but in that time, youth and life assert themselves and you will be able to give your heart again but in a much fuller, deeper sense."

Amanda looked at Sara. If anyone else had said these words, she would have dismissed them without a thought as the easy advice of one who had neither loved deeply nor suffered much. Yet she knew Sara had been orphaned, then widowed. Amanda was understanding enough to realize that Sara spoke with heartfelt sincerity out of the depth of her own painful experiences. "Thank you, I know it must be hard for you to say these things to me and I do appreciate your kindness. I will remember what you have said to me here today."

The two women embraced and a few tears were shared in the sunlight. After a while they got up and were strolling idly toward the rose garden when Gussie and Mr. Ames came around the corner of the arbor. The sunlight gilded their hair and Amanda gave a gasp of pleasure. "Oh, what a splendid couple they make!" Sara smiled agreement and they were soon joined by the other two.

Mr. Ames made his bows and asked them if they thought they would be up to a short jaunt the next day. He had taken a house near Pickstowe he said, ". . . so I can keep an eye on you ladies over the next few weeks. I am practicing being an uncle, so as not to disgrace you when we come to be related." He gave his ready grin. The ladies thought his idea of luncheon at Carding Manor was a pleasant way to spend the day and fell in with the plan.

"Then I'll be over about eleven o'clock for you," Mr.

Ames replied, pleased. Although Gussie pressed him to stay and lunch with them, Christopher Ames pleaded business and left with the sentiment that he would eagerly await the morrow.

CHAPTER TWELVE

"That," Augusta said, looking up from her embroidery, "was quite the noisiest game of chess I have ever heard. I am more used to tense silences with only an occasional monosyllable uttered in wrath!"

"Ah, but that is because you have been used to players who knew what they were doing!" Sara chuckled. "I have never played so ill in my life. I advanced into the jaws of defeat when I should have retreated. I retreated when I should have marched on to victory. An unbelievable muddle!"

"And *I*," Amanda laughed, "have been even worse. There is nothing for it but to go to my room and think about my misguided playing." Here she yawned daintily behind her little hand, but Sara spotted it.

"Rather, you should go to your room and have a nap,

for we've both been yawning over the board the past twenty minutes; I shall go and lie down a while myself," Sara said as she put the carved pieces back into their velvet-lined box. She stood up, stretched and then left to follow her own advice.

Once in her room, however, Sara found her thoughts again returning to Lord Ramsey. Damn the man! Whenever her mind was not fully occupied, he was there, haunting her. She fled the seclusion of her room, stopping only to pick up her water-color gear. In moments she was out on the lawn, capturing the loveliness of a summer's day in the country.

The evening was spent quietly after an early supper. Sara read aloud while Augusta and Amanda did their needlework. As the three indulged in a walk down to the lake by moonlight, Sara reflected that life seemed to be returning to its proper balance. The day had passed pleasantly. And if there were no high spots, neither were there any low ones. She stoutly refused to dwell on the notion that this comfortable, this safe life might be very boring after a few days.

The next morning Augusta and Amanda went into the town of Pickstowe to pick up some ribbons and other sundries. Their errand accomplished, they walked along the cobbled incline to where a little Norman church stood, its square tower boldly challenging the dark yews growing around it. Inside, Gussie exclaimed over the carved stone memorials on either side and had stopped to read every historical plaque and marker. The damp and gloom cast a pall over Amanda. With a word to Augusta she was off through the side door that led into the quiet churchyard with its crooked rows of old slabs and occasional ornate marble markers. She found the place not oppressive, but strangely comforting.

As she rounded the corner of the church, she almost

collided with Binghampton, who with his friend Mr. Cranshaw, was traversing the mossy path to the church door. While Bing and Amanda stared at each other in speechless surprise, Mr. Cranshaw, being exempt from this affliction, was inspired to utter flowery phrases.

"Fair vision, be you angel or ghost? If either, I would die willingly that I might rest my eyes on you forever!" He removed his hat and swept Amanda a courtly bow.

"Don't be such a dunderhead, George!" Binghampton muttered as he too made his bow to the lady.

"Why, Lord Binghampton! You are the last person I would expect to see here," Amanda said, mortified by the rosy blush that suffused her face.

"She speaks! 'Tis an angel after all," Cranshaw emoted, receiving a quelling look from his companion. "But do you know this divine creature? Lucky mortal! Let me but know her name and I am enslaved for life, nay eternity!" he insisted, not being one to discourage easily.

Lord Binghampton eyed his friend with something akin to dislike. "Go to the devil, George!" he muttered in a tone that brooked no argument. "I'll catch up with you later." The unfortunate Mr. Cranshaw left reluctantly after sweeping Amanda another bow.

The two left standing on the path eyed each other almost warily. "Would you like to sit on that bench over in the sunshine?" Bing suggested. Amanda noded and he took her hand and placed it on his arm as he escorted her to the carved stone bench.

"What pleasant weather," she remarked as she seated herself.

"Yes, it has been very fine!" Binghampton conceded heartily. A silence fell.

"Are you staying here or just passing through..." they both began at once. Amanda dimpled.

"My brother and I do that often!" she said. "We are

forever starting to say the same thing at the same time."
Binghampton frowned at being compared to a brother, and
returned to the subject on his mind.

"Are you visiting with friends here? I thought you to
still be in London enjoying the height of the Season."

Amanda, who hoped but very much doubted that he
had any particular thought to her whereabouts when not
in her immediate vicinity, blushed again and looked down
at her gloves.

"I am staying at Laurel House with Mrs. Roche and
Sara Roche for a few weeks. They have taken the house
so Sara can convalesce away from the noise and heat of
London, for she has been quite ill, you know."

"No, I did not know that and am very sorry to hear it.
I've been staying with my friend Mr. Cranshaw since last
week. I, er . . . wasn't very nice to him just now, but
. . . I rather wanted to keep you to myself after not seeing
you in such a long while."

Amanda rose to her feet. "Lord Binghampton, you
know it . . . isn't proper to address such remarks to me
when we are alone." She started back to the church. "I
must rejoin Mrs. Roche."

Binghampton looked at her in dismay, as the elation
he had felt on seeing her so unexpectedly changed to concern.

"Miss Bensome! I have the feeling that I have inad-
vertently offended. Please tell me what I have done that
I might make amends!"

"Oh! No! I mean of course not! I mean you could
apologize if you had offended, but indeed you have not!
Oh dear!" she exclaimed, her thoughts as tangled as her
tongue.

Binghampton seemed not to notice. He took her hand
in his and smiled widely. "Then I may call on you at
Laurel House?"

"Yes! No! I mean there is no need . . . so kind . . ."
She struggled to say what she thought she meant, but
Augusta came out into the churchyard just at that moment.

"So there you are! Why, Lord Binghampton, how nice
to see you again," Gussie said smoothly, holding out her
hand to him. Amanda's blushing shyness and Bing's apparent bewilderment told her all she needed to know. "I
hope you will call on us at Laurel House while you are
in the area! It is so pleasant to meet one's friends and
acquaintances when one is rusticating away from the hustle
and bustle of town life."

Lord Binghampton correctly interpreted this to mean
that Augusta Roche, at least, was quickly finding that
occupying her charges during their country sojourn might
become a wearisome task without some diversion, and
accepted the invitation.

"If you will be home this afternoon I will do myself
the honor of calling on you and paying my respects to
Madame Roche also," he said, a hopeful note in his voice.

"We shall be gone *all* afternoon, visiting with friends
in the neighborhood," Gussie answered, assessing the effect of these words on the young lord. She hoped that
Binghampton might remember that Lord Trowbridge, who
had been dangling after Amanda, lived nearby. "Tomorrow, perhaps!" she suggested, pleased with the way his
face had stiffened somewhat.

"Tomorrow, then. I shall be looking forward to it," he
said and offered to escort the two ladies back to their
carriage. While they sauntered back up the street to the
inn where the groom had waited with the equipage the two
younger members of the party were fairly quiet, not offering any conversation except in reply to Gussie's comments. As he handed Amanda up into the carriage, Binghampton's hand held hers perhaps a trifle too long.

Realizing this, she hurriedly pulled it from his grasp on the pretext of settling her reticule on the seat.

Harboring the darkest thoughts concerning Lord Trowbridge, Lord Binghampton made his way to the tap room of the inn and joined his friend. Mr. Cranshaw was sulky at first but his sense of humor was restored at the diverting picture of the usually sunny-tempered Bing glowering into his ale.

"I say, you look like a thunderhead!" Mr. Cranshaw laughed as Binghampton took a hearty pull at his brew, scowling fiercely. "No, now that I get a good look, more like a *hound*!" The young man laughed at his own sally, but his companion failed to respond to this good-natured railery. "By Jove," Cranshaw said in surprise, "this has the appearance of a serious business!" He eyed Binghampton thoughtfully. "What's the problem? No dowry? Shouldn't think *you* would stick at that, no matter how your family might cut up!"

"Lord, no!" Bing replied. "As if that would matter a button! I'm as warm as any man," he said indignantly.

"Then what's to do? You can't say that she's indifferent to you, not the way she colored-up and dropped her eyes every time she looked up at you!" At these words Binghampton's countenance lightened.

"You know, your brother's all wrong about you, George! Damned if you're not a good man!" And with this back-handed praise and a clap on the shoulder, Binghampton ordered another round for himself and his "very good friend, George!"

By late afternoon the two young men were in prime twig, very mellow indeed. "By God, George, if you weren't so cow-handed, I'd put you up for membership in the Four-Horse Club!"

George, knowing his limitations as a whipster, was still

almost overcome by this supreme accolade of his friend, and the two went off arm in arm in the best of spirits.

Amanda, however, remained fairly agitated for the rest of the day. She had left London determined to put the dashing Lord Binghampton out of her mind and now to have him turn up almost on her very doorstep was more than she could bear. She took a stroll along the drive with Sara and unburdened her heart.

"I know that he is very eligible and someone like myself very gauche and beneath his touch. Once I had made up my mind to the facts it was easier for me to see him in Society without such wrenching of my feelings, but now that he is here in Pickstowe and there will not be other people around to act as buffers . . . I know I won't be able to carry it off."

"I will do all I can to help, my dear," Sara promised. "Tomorrow just leave the conversation to me and I will steer it in familiar channels so your mind can be made easier."

"Oh, that will be such a help. And after we return to London, except for certain of the balls and routs it will be easy to avoid him. Oh, Sara! Would you think me terribly craven if I said I had the headache tomorrow and didn't come down?"

"My dear Amanda, that would be much worse! Then you would dread every dance and party for fear he would come on the scene. It's best to get over rough ground lightly. Have courage!" Sara cringed a little at her own hypocrisy, for while she had no doubt that her advice to Amanda was the best, she had no intention of following it in her own case.

During the long morning while Augusta and Amanda had been in town, Sara had forged her future plans. She liked the little town and the sleepy village well enough, but thought perhaps something near the coast would be more suitable. A small country house, well away from any principal city, would be ideal, for she could devote herself to her neglected landscape painting and live nicely indeed on the investments from the monies she had earned with her portraits.

"What a contemptible coward I am, urging Amanda to face the music while I want to flee from my own feelings!" Sara was eventually able to convince herself that since Amanda was in the first bloom of youth and would most likely find an eligible and agreeable suitor in the near future, that their cases were dissimilar enough to warrant differing responses. After all, some young man would offer Amanda his hand in marriage, while Ramsey...what could he offer? Not marriage, for he was already betrothed to the stunningly lovely Lady Pamela Kennerly; and yet his amorous pursuit left Sara with no doubt as to his passionate feelings for her.

What then could his actions mean? Sara had tried not to analyze this, but in the back of her mind lurked the fear that Ramsey, knowing something of her history and the dreadful duel that had left both Jerome and Alfred dead on Finchley Common, might have misconstrued her character. Certainly her fervent responses might have given him justifiable cause, she thought.

Well, his intentions were neither here nor there, and whether the Earl meant to offer her a *carte blanche*, or whether he had only a casual dalliance in mind it could make no difference, since Sara fully intended never to see him again. She turned her thoughts in other directions by force of mind, and was busily making plans for her future country residence.

A small house, possibly late Tudor or Queen Anne, placed on a height and near the sea. The furnishings from the house on Green Dolphin Street would fit in more with the later style, and Sara would not have to redo all the furnishings if she took an unfurnished place. And definitely some spare bedrooms with vistas of the sea or woods so that the future Mrs. Ames and her family would have a place to stay with Sara whenever they returned to England and the attractions of town life palled.

While Sara made her plans, Amanda was also preparing for the future. Certain she would never love any other man as she did Lord Binghampton, she was dispassionately assessing her current suitors. She liked Sir Harvey Moreton and found his companionship pleasant if unexciting. Believing she could never return his regard with the force he deserved, she put him aside. Captain Harrington of the Guards was handsome and lively company, but not at all eligible and rather too flamboyant for her quiet tastes. That left Lord Trowbridge.

While not of her generation, Lord Trowbridge was still of an age to be considered a good match for Amanda, despite the fact that he had two children, one of them his heir who was presently at Eton. His estates were well-managed, his reputation good and his face and figure were generally thought to be quite pleasing. Not a few lures had been thrown out his way and the Society matrons had looked with approval on his partiality for Miss Bensome.

And how pleased her mama and papa would be! To have her married off in her first Season would be quite a relief to her parents with so many children to send into the fashionable world. As with all girls of her age and station, Amanda had been trained from birth to be a wife. Besides the management of a household, in which she was well versed, her only requirements were to be pleasant, obedient and dutiful and conduct herself as a lady of quality in Society. That she was also pretty and graceful were bonuses almost certain to insure an eligible attachment for her.

After thinking the matter through, Amanda decided that

it would have to be Lord Trowbridge, but neither his good looks and kindness nor his material possessions had any real bearing on the decision. She knew that while he admired her and with the slightest encouragement would make her the mistress of his estates and stepmother to his children, he was not at all in love with her. This was only fair, since she was not in the least in love with him, and indeed, love was not looked for in the marriages of her class. Respect would grow and affection might someday follow, and after all, who was she to expect more than was her due? Besides, she did so love children!

With these thoughts Amanda found a good deal of comfort, and since Sara also felt once more in control of her life, dinner at Laurel House was a gayer affair than the previous evening. Augusta, seeing Amanda's face relieved of the strain of the past few days, attributed this to Binghampton's arrival in town and was more determined than ever to take a hand in the affair.

The three ladies walked down the drive together to meet Mr. Ames who had promised to ride over for a few rubbers of whist. When he turned into the drive, he was pleasantly surprised to see all three who came to greet him were looking cheerful with their eyes bright and cheeks reflecting the glow of health.

"What, three beautiful nymphs to greet me! Surely I'm the most fortunate man in Pickstowe!" he exclaimed with an expectant look. Gussie did not disappoint him.

"In Pickstowe!" his intended remonstrated in mock indignation. "How unhandsome of you, Christopher!"

"Did I say Pickstowe?" he countered. "Of course, I meant in all of England!" He dropped down from his mount to walk up the drive with the ladies.

"Speaking of nymphs, when can we expect Janie to join you? She is coming some time this week, is she not?" Gussie asked, unaware of the sinking sensation Amanda experienced at these words, for they offered a ready explanation for Lord Binghampton's presence in the area.

"Yes," Mr. Ames answered. "She has been under the wing of my cousin, Lady Staple, and will be coming down by the end of the week. They have been to Arundel. I expect to hear that the entire party got lost in those endless halls and only Janie's skill at tracking kept them from starvation in some drafty corridor!" He was rewarded by a burst of laughter from his companions.

The conversation continued in this tone throughout the evening. The American's droll humor was a tonic. They talked and played whist until Polly brought the tea tray in a half hour after nine; an hour later Christopher Ames was riding down the drive on his strapping bay.

CHAPTER THIRTEEN

Christopher had not been gone above fifteen minutes, and the ladies of Laurel House were just ascending the stairway to the bedroom floor, when the sound of a stringed instrument coming from the garden drew their attention. The music drifted in through open drawing-room windows, and the ladies retraced their steps to seek out the source.

On the flagged terrace in the moonlight stood a man dressed in gipsy garb, but much finer and cleaner than sported by any Romany ever seen in the neighborhood. He held a fiddle beneath his chin and the rings on his fingers and hanging from his ears gleamed in the silvery light as he brought the bow across the strings in a plaintive melody. Witherall was standing nearby but his stance was relaxed so Sara knew they were in no danger from the stranger. As the ladies came forward to the window, the gipsy bowed to each of them, reserving his most elaborate bow for Gussie. Then he raised his bowstring again and played the old ballad of the "Gipsy Rover" with great gusto.

Sara saw that Augusta's eyes were twinkling with mischief, and when the musician had finished his piece, Gussie allowed that it was the most discordant and untuneful sawing at strings she had ever heard.

At this evaluation, the gipsy raised his head and pushed his bandanna back with the hand that held the bowstring. "And to think you called *my* remarks 'unhandsome' earlier this evening!" said a laughing voice which belonged to no one else but the indomitable American.

Sara and Amanda praised his playing, and Gussie admitted that she had recognized him almost from the start. This cheered the fiddler so much that he played them a rousing chorus of "Yankee Doodle," explaining that was so his bride could get accustomed to some "good American rhythm." Then he took his leave for the second and final time of the evening and went to retrieve his horse which he had hidden in the adjoining wood.

At breakfast the next morning the talk was of the irrepressible American and his moonlight serenade. "How marvelous to discover a new and quite unexpected talent in one's intended husband," Augusta said, laughing. "Although I am beginning to wonder if I will find myself in a country of eccentrics!"

With tongue in cheek, Sara affectionately voiced her opinion that Gussie would fit in well. "Indeed," she then added sincerely, "I have rarely seen two people who suit so well." The talk changed to which gowns they would wear to luncheon at Carding Manor, and before they knew it, it was time to depart.

They reached their destination in good time, and after

a delightful *al fresco* meal in the extensive formal garden
at the manor, were shown about the grounds by their host.
There were several unusual shrubs and plants and there
was even a small maze with yews clipped into geometric
forms and archways leading from one area to another.
Gussie and Mr. Ames managed to get lost from the rest
of the party for a few minutes and they emerged smiling
and flushed, but except for exchanging conspiratory winks
the other two pretended not to notice.

The afternoon went by so quickly that Sara exclaimed
when she heard the time, but Amanda was secretly hopeful
that Lord Binghampton would have paid his courtesy call
while they were out. She did not think that he would care
to wait till their return or bother come back a second time.
In this she wronged him, for when they returned to Laurel
House, arriving shortly after their normal teatime, it was
to meet Witherall's announcement that a guest was waiting
in the small parlor. Sara went at once and found Lord
Binghampton sipping a glass of port and staring morosely
at the wallpaper with its pattern of tiny gilded birdcages
filled with flowers.

"Pray forgive us, my lord, but we have been lunching
with . . . a friend . . ." she said truthfully, leaving Binghampton to fill in the pauses as he might. "The time went
by so pleasantly that in less congenial company, we might
have been thought to have overstayed our welcome!"
These words evidently had their desired effect, for the
sight of the young man's somber face perked up Sara
enormously. "Aunt Augusta and Miss Bensome will be
down as soon as they have freshened up, for you must
know that traipsing all over a country house that is not
regularly surveyed by the lady of the manor can be quite
a dusty affair. Of course there is no lady of the house, and
since the gentleman has only recently come down from

London the servants have taken advantage of the situation."

Not knowing Sara well, Binghampton could not realize that it was not her wont to criticize the housekeeping habits of her friends with her acquaintances. He stood looking at the carpet for a few seconds, then raised his head.

"You must be perfectly frank with me, I beg you, madame! Am I too late with my suit . . ." He turned and looked his hostess in the eye with such intensity that Sara was gratified she was on the right track.

"If she has consented to be the wife of a man old enough to be her father! If I have lost the only woman I will ever love by my backwardness I will never forgive myself!" he declared.

Sara forgave him his histrionics for the blazing sincerity in his eyes, and deciding it would be cruel to toy with such a gallant fish any longer, chose a more direct strategy.

"Forgive me! Your speech is not quite coherent; is it Miss Bensome you are speaking of?" she asked innocently.

"Who else in all the world can it be? I have not been myself since that wretched balloon ascension, all because of . . . Amanda!"

"Well, it appears to me that you have a rather strange way of courting a young lady: one day you are all attention, the next you hardly come near her. And it seems to me that a few short weeks ago you formed a noticeable part of Miss Ames's court; as one of Miss Bensome's sponsors and in the absence of her parents, I would be very remiss if I didn't question the strength of your professed attachment for her," Sara replied, fighting to keep a smile out of her voice: the resultant grimace of severity was all the young lord needed to cast himself in the most despicable light.

"I cannot blame you for thinking me a flighty fellow,

but please hear me out! When I met Miss Ames I was dazzled by her beauty and her interesting American ways; and to be honest, since half the young men of my acquaintance threw themselves at her feet . . . well, one does not want to seem to be out of the swim of things after all!" This very young, very honest revelation was almost the undoing of his listener, but the earnestness of the situation helped Sara maintain her poise as he continued.

"When I sat next to Miss Bensome at the balloon ascension and looked down into her sweet little face I thought for a moment that one of their sandbags had hit me!" Bing stated, causing Sara to choke a bit.

"Oh, I don't blame you for thinking I exaggerate," he went on, mistaking the sound of her smothered mirth for a disapproving noise. "I went home in a positive daze, but after that I was very unsure of my feelings; I began to wonder if my character might be *fickle*!" he related with horror. "I knew that Ama . . . Miss Bensome was very shy and special and I wanted to make very sure of the emotions I labored under before putting myself forward. I wouldn't do anything in the world to hurt her! You must believe me! Oh, how can I convince you?" he said despairingly.

"It is not I, but Amanda and her parents you must convince, if you wish to offer for her hand," Sara advised.

"You mean . . . you mean she has not accepted Trowbridge yet?" Binghampton cried in relief.

"No, she had not accepted Trowbridge yet," Sara answered obliquely, telling herself that it was, after all, only the truth!

"Thank God! Then do I have your permission to speak to Ama . . . Miss Bensome to find out if she would favor my suit?" He took Sara's hand in his and pressed in warmly.

Smiling, she said, "I will go up and ask her if she will speak to you here." She went slowly up the stairs, thoughtfully stopping along the way to admire the lusters in the hall chandelier, and to smell the roses in the cloisonné bowl on the landing and even to spend a few minutes looking out the mullioned window at the back of the landing to see if there appeared a likelihood of rain. Satisfied at last, Sara knocked lightly on Amanda's door. Sara noted approvingly that her charge looked particularly lovely in a tea gown of watered primrose silk with a froth of lace at the collar and cuffs.

"You look charming, my dear," she said. "Will you help entertain our guest while I freshen up a bit? Oh, heavens! I left my reticule in the sitting room. Would you mind fetching it for me?" Sara had left her reticule there with this request in mind.

Amanda was only too happy to comply since she felt it would put off the moment of facing Lord Binghampton a little longer. As she left, Sara gave a glance heavenward and sincerely hoped she might be excused her dissembling in the name of love.

Amanda tiptoed past the drawing-room door which was closed to her vast relief, and passed on down the hall to the sitting-room door which was also closed. Had she been less nervous, it might have struck her as unusual to have closed the doors on a guest in such warm weather when every little breeze was encouraged. As it was, she opened the door and was inside before she noted Binghampton standing rather rigidly by the mantelpiece.

"You!" she exclaimed inelegantly. Lord Binghampton came forward and grasped her hand tightly, as she seemed to be on the point of fleeing.

"How are you, Miss Bensome?" the young man said. "But I need not ask for I have never seen you in better looks!"

She attempted to pull her hand loose from his firm grasp, and trying to think of something casual to say, blurted out the first thing to come to her mind. "How . . . how is Miss Ames?" she asked, her eyes wide and blue as forget-me-nots.

"Miss Ames! How do I know how Miss Ames does?" Binghampton answered in surprise. "I may hope she does well, but I didn't come here to talk of Miss Ames!"

"Oh! Then . . . how is your dear mama?" She asked, groping for anything to say.

"The devil take . . . er, my mother is well, thank you," the young man corrected himself quickly. "And so are my father and sister and young brother and all my aunts and uncles and cousins!"

"I beg your pardon?" Amanda asked in surprised, looking so utterly sweet and adorable that Binghampton had swept her into his arms and planted an off-center kiss on her soft lips before she even knew what had happened. She struggled and pushed him away but he held her fast.

"Sir!" she cried, "Have you taken leave of your senses?" Tears started in her eyes. "Let go of me at once."

"Yes, I have taken leave of my senses since I met you. I don't know up from down, here from there. And no, I will not let you go until you tell me that you do *not* love that old dotard, Trowbridge; and that you will do me the honor of becoming my wife."

"He is not an old dotard! . . . What!" Amanda exclaimed as his last words registered in her brain.

"You cannot love him!" Lord Binghampton declared and he bent his head and kissed her determinedly and thoroughly. When he released his embrace a bit, Amanda reached up and put her arms about his neck, caressing the back of it where the hair curled gently at the nape.

"Of course I cannot love him, when I have loved you almost from the moment I saw you!" she sighed, smiling so fetchingly that Bing was obliged to kiss her again.

"I am so unworthy to be loved by you, but my adored

one, I promise you will never regret being my wife! I love you with all my heart."

While the two young lovers professed their vows of love, Gussie descended the staircase and joined Sara in the drawing room. "Why, has Lord Binghampton taken his leave? And where is Amanda?"

"I expect they will be joining us soon. If not, we shall have to go fetch them," Sara observed laughing, "for, if I am not mistaken, he is making a declaration at this very moment."

"Famous!" Augusta chuckled with a clap of her hands. "Now, my dear, if we could only see you happily married everything would be perfect!"

"Dear Aunt, I can be perfectly happy without being married. In fact, I have done so for some years now, and intend to remain in my state of single blessedness," Sara responded with perfect truth.

"You know that is not what I meant, child; why, if I hadn't met Christopher, I would never have married again for it was very pleasant being independent and my own mistress; still, once I met him I knew I would never be so contented again if I refused his love and companionship."

"Yes, it would have been wrong to have done so. I'm convinced the two of you were truly destined for each other. If he had not decided to bring his daughter out in London, if Amanda had not come to stay with us, if he had not sought to have his daughter's portrait done; so much had to come together! It seems fate took a hand in your plans," Sara concluded.

"That is true. I've thought about it in that light myself," Gussie admitted with a glowing smile. "But if fate is interested in the life of Augusta Roche, why not also in the life of *Sara* Roche? Since…since Jerome died, have you never truly met another man you might love?" Gussie inquired gently. "I don't mean to intrude on your privacy," she added seeing the quick shadow that clouded Sara's countenance, "but you are so...so alive, so passionately alive and so beautiful and intelligent! Somewhere, surely, there is a man worthy of your heart and hand!"

"Once...a certain gentleman...I could have... but he was not eligible and it would not have worked in any case. My heart was not . . . much . . . involved," Sara said looking down abstractedly, tracing a line on the carpet with the toe of her slipper.

"I am so sorry! Please forgive me, Sara, but I only asked out of my affection and concern for you."

At this moment, they were interrupted by the door opening. Amanda and Lord Binghampton appeared hesitantly in the doorway. Binghampton's cravat was crushed and Amanda's fair hair had escaped in little tendrils that drifted against her cheeks and the back of her neck. All this along with their sparkling eyes and flushed cheeks told the story even before they spoke.

"Mrs. Roche, Madame Roche, I have come to ask for leave to pay my addresses to Ama...Miss Bensome. I will go to Hampshire on Saturday to ask formal permission of her parents!" he announced proudly.

"Amanda, does this meet with your approval? If not, we will send Lord Binghampton away with a flea in his ear!" Gussie asked, barely keeping a straight face.

"Oh, no! Do not do *that*!" a horrified Amanda cried out.

"We have absolutely *no* intention of doing that." Sara laughed as she came forward and embraced the girl. "I wish you both very happy!"

"As do I!" Gussie added in congratulation. "And while I can foresee no objections, I will promise to do what I can to promote your suit," she told the elated young man. "Now if you two would like to take a turn in the garden, you will have just enough time before dinner is announced."

The two happy young people went with alacrity, and when they were out of sight Gussie and Sara hugged each other. "They will deal extremely well together!" Augusta announced satisfactorily. "Two weddings! What great fun!"

"I feel very badly that my untimely illness caused you to postpone your banns."

"Nonsense! I have enjoyed having a few more weeks of courtship before we settle down as stodgy married folks."

"Stodgy! You and Christopher?" Sara hooted in a most unladylike manner. "I would like to see *that* day, but fear I'll be long in my grave before it ever happens."

A few minutes later the gentleman in question came cantering up the drive on his large bay. As his intended greeted him, he held out a nosegay that he had carried inside his coat, and presented it to his love with a bow.

"How lovely," Gussie began, then she exclaimed, "How . . . good Lord, are these for me?"

"Do you think I offer jewels to all the women of my acquaintance?" her fiancé laughed. "What a very curious man you must think me, my love!"

"But . . . oh! They are gorgeous!" the incredulous Gussie whispered.

"What, speechless!" Mr. Ames declared. "Let me take them away if they have overset you so much!" he said with one of his famous grins, but Gussie refused to surrender her treasure.

Nestled in a cone of white paper lace and surrounded by fern branches was a bouquet of gems in gold settings composed of a necklace, earrings, brooch, bracelet, ring and hair spray of richly glowing red rubies, diamonds and baroque pearls set in flower shapes.

"These are the Ames's family jewels," he added, his hazel eyes twinkling.

"They are fabulous!" Gussie breathed. "Have they been in your family long?"

Mr. Ames pulled out his gold watch and flicked open the cover. "Oh, about two hours," he replied nonchalantly although his eyes were brimming with laughter. "Rogers just posted down from London with them today. Are you pleased? I designed them just for you, so they aren't 'family' jewels at all; more of an engagement token."

"*You* designed them?" an astonished Gussie asked. "Will you never stop surprising me with your talents?!"

"Well, I certainly hope not!" Mr. Ames replied. "Shall we take a tour of the garden?" he asked with a romantic light in his eye.

"Well, not the garden." Gussie laughed at the way his face fell. "But perhaps the shrubbery . . . ?"

Christopher Ames took her arm and they strolled off arm-in-arm past the laurels while she filled him in on the day's events. In the course of their conversation Gussie mentioned her concern for Sara, "for she has some maggot in her head about finding a home somewhere in the country and living there year-round. She has evidently developed a *tendre* for some ineligible gentleman, and fearing to bruise her heart once more, is determined to flee from any chance of meeting him again. Oh! If only I had some idea who he might be!" she said feelingly.

Mr. Ames was quiet for a moment, then said, "I fancy I have a good idea who the gentleman may be. Has she ever spoken of Lord Ramsey to you?"

"Ramsey! No, indeed she has rarely mentioned him at all. How strange! You may be right, my love," she sighed. "Now *there* is a man!"

"Oh," said Christopher Ames, taking Gussie in his arms and kissing her soundly. "Should I be jealous already?"

"No," Gussie replied, matching her actions to prove her words.

After a while they returned to the house for dinner and joined Sara, Amanda and Binghampton who awaited them in the airy dining room. The meal was informal and since Amanda and Lord Binghampton, who now answered happily to his Christian name of Robert, were so rapt in their golden clouds of sentiment, the course of the conversation was readily turned to an astute Mr. Ames.

The American talked of the news from London, regaled them with the several of the less scandalous *on-dits* of Society and mentioned a set of matched greys he had purchased at Tattersall's. Then he casually introduced Ramsey's name, saying that he had seen him at the horse sale and that the debonair Earl seemed in no way put out by the breakup of his engagement. "Oh, I beg pardon, Binghampton!" the American said, as if just remembering that Lady Pamela Kennerly was the sister of the young lord.

Binghampton, distracted by the continued nearness of his soon-to-be fiancée was very offhand about the matter. "It's not as if it was a love match on either side," he said, "unless you consider Pamela's love of his title! I like Ramsey too well to see him saddled with—" He stopped, realizing his indiscretion, and blushed redly, but Augusta intervened, changing the conversation to a story she had heard about the Countess of Lapham and the manuevering it took to get that lady's second daughter a marriageable husband. The company laughed at the shenanigans Gussie related, until it was time for the ladies to retire to the drawing room.

Bowing to time-honored tradition, Mr. Ames sat over some excellent port with Lord Binghampton, and was again able to direct the conversation in the direction of his choice. After talking about the coming hunting season and comparing it to Virginia, the Amercian returned to the subject of Ramsey.

"A bruising rider, I've heard. I collect he's a great friend of yours?"

"Yes," Binghampton answered, reddening again. "That's why I almost put my foot in my mouth, boot and all, at dinner! I like Ned too well to see him miserable, and that's what would have happened. As a matter of fact, I like you too well for that, and for a while I thought you were interested in my sister also," he continued with a question in his voice.

"A beautiful girl, and she can be very charming. Not my cup of tea. I like a high-spirited woman with a few more years on her than your sister has. Rather like the difference between spring wine and fine aged brandy!" he declared, thinking of Augusta.

"Well, I wish you happy, sir," Binghampton said, and he raised his glass to toast the coming nuptials of Augusta Roche and Christopher Ames.

In turn, Mr. Ames, saluted the engagement soon to be announced between Miss Bensome and Lord Binghampton. After exchanging a few more, the two gentlemen were feeling quite mellow.

"Strange we were talking about Ramsey," Bing mentioned as the thought struck him. "Why, I just ran into him a few days ago. He lit out of London about the same time I did, unbeknownst to me. Ran into him at the inn near Lymestoke Wednesday when I stopped for an ale. Been staying at his place near Upper Lymestoke," he added.

"Is he still there?" questioned the American, sitting up a little more attentively.

"Why, he said he had a mind to stay there all summer. It's where he grew up, you know, except when he stayed with the late Earl of Ramsey Park."

"How far is it to Upper Lymestoke from Pickstowe?" Mr. Ames asked intently.

"Only about an easy hour and a half," a surprised but slightly muzzy Binghampton replied. "Perhaps less. Going to visit him?"

"No, but someone I know is going to pay him a visit shortly." Christopher smiled broadly. "If you'll join the ladies, I'll be with you in a moment." He rang the bell for Witherall.

When Binghampton left and the butler came in answer to the summons, Mr. Ames rose and walked over to the mantelpiece. "Witherall, you are devoted to your mistress," he stated rather than asked.

"Yes, sir, that is correct." Witherall maintained his aloof demeanor and hid his curiosity.

"And you would do anything to insure her happiness," the American continued.

Witherall replied, "Of course, sir," in suave but heartfelt tones.

"Then would you undertake a task for me that I think would insure that happiness? It would involve . . . a short journey, and a bit of . . . thespian talent. But I fancy you're no stranger to the boards?" Mr. Ames smiled at the astonishment on Witherall's face.

"If it is for the good of Madame Roche, I will do anything, even to the laying down of my life!" the butler-cum-actor emoted.

"I sincerely doubt it will come to that, but it will possibly involve . . . *implying* something that is no longer so. I think I can trust it to your talents, however!"

And promising to make his absence good with Mrs. Augusta Roche, the American filled Witherall in on his plan.

When he joined Binghampton and the ladies in the drawing room, he managed to get Augusta aside long enough to whisper a brief description of his plot and gain her cooperation. Since Binghampton and Amanda were so engrossed in their new-found joy, Mr. Ames had no difficulty in setting up for a very late evening, going so far as to have Gussie arrange to have the tea tray brought in at a later time to aid in the illusion that not as much time had passed.

Then the American went to the piano near the open doors and amazed his audience by thundering out a chorus of wild operatic music which completely obliterated the sound of his horse being led quietly through the trees that bordered the drive. In a few minutes Witherall, dressed properly as a groom despite his longing to put on the guise of a highwayman, was galloping along the road to Upper Lymestoke.

After a few miles Witherall slowed his horse to an easy canter and enjoyed the ride through the quiet country roads and lanes in the light of the full moon. After obtaining more explicit directions in Lymestock, he spurred his mount to a gallop, and timing it nicely, he continued looking appropriately disheveled and heated on a well-lathered horse when he reached his destination.

He mounted the front steps and with great glee loudly banged out an ominous tattoo with the heavy brass knocker. When a sleepy-eyed manservant answered the repeated summons, Witherall demanded in his most dramatic accents that he see the Earl of Ramsey immediately. He adamantly refused to give the sealed letter he bore into any other hand, and at last the harassed servant let Witherall into the darkened hall, muttering that his master had only just gone to bed.

After a span of only a few minutes a half-asleep and highly irritated Lord Ramsey descended the carved staircase wrapped in a dark red velvet robe. He was about to demand an explanation, when Witherall stepped closer to the candelabra and was recognized.

"Witherton?" he questioned, taking the last three steps in a leap. "What on earth is this all about!"

Witherall, for once not bothering to correct his latest assumed name, rolled his eyes in a look of mortal distress and asserted that his instructions were to deliver the message privately. With a suspicious frown, the Earl assented and led the way to his library. He turned and demanded again to know what was going on.

In reply Witherall handed him the sealed missive with its hastily scrawled direction. Ramsey tore open the envelope and read the single line enclosed.

I must see you immediately on an urgent matter regarding Mdme. Sara Roche.

It bore the simple signature, "Ames."

"Is there no more? What is wrong?" the Earl demanded hoarsely. "My God! Has something happened to her?!"

Witherall allowed his eyes to mist with tears and managed to let one single drop spill slowly down his cheek. "Madame has been very ill, my lord," he said simply.

"How ill, damn it?" Ramsey cried out.

"We have been in fear for her life, my lord," the messenger replied with absolute, if no longer current, truth.

Ramsey pulled so violently on the bell cord that he was in danger of bringing the contraption down about his ears. In a few terse sentences he ordered his racing curricle brought around, refreshments for Witherall and care for his horse, and disappeared to change into traveling dress.

A gratified Witherall was led around to the kitchen where the sympathetic housekeeper and the cook plied him with hot coffee, thick sliced roast beef and tender crusty bread and some very good ale. By the time he was restored, he almost believed that he had ridden a great distance at much danger to his life and limb in order to summon Lord Ramsey on a mission of mercy. The fact that the cook's brown eyes became as round as dinner plates and the housekeeper herself went to fetch a tot of whiskey to marshal his flagging energies added to his satisfaction. "H' ain't lost m' tetch, by God!" he muttered happily.

CHAPTER FOURTEEN

Quicker than could be expected, Ramsey was back down the stairs and into his curricle which awaited him at the door with his two new dapple greys harnessed and fretting to be off. Leaving Witherall to follow, the Earl went down the drive at a brisk trot, and when he reached the road he gave the horses their heads. They were fresh and feisty and with his light hand on the reins Ramsey arrived in Pickstowe in just under an hour. Shortly after, he was bowling up the driveway to Laurel House, to where fate, in the person of Christopher Jonathan Ames, awaited him.

The hostessess and guests at Laurel House had just partaken of late refreshments. Mr. Ames, with Gussie's help, had managed to keep the little party from breaking up. The sound of horses surprised Sara but Mr. Ames, exchanging a wink with Gussie, was on his feet and out into the hallway, closing the door carefully behind him. Thus he was able to intercept the Earl before he had reached the door.

Ramsey, throwing his reins to a bewildered stableboy, jumped down from his curricle and took the stairs at a bound, his heart thumping more painfully than it had when he had been cornered once in the Peninsula. He had the same sick feeling in the pit of his stomach, as the door swung open before him. He was inside before the American caused him to check by saying "Slow down! There is no need for such haste."

"What word of her?" Ramsey cried. "She is . . . she is not . . . gone!"

"No," replied Mr. Ames smoothly. "Right now she's in the drawing room taking tea with her aunt and some guests."

"Is this some kind of mad jest!" the Earl exploded. "What is the meaning of this?!"

"If you'll lower your voice and join me in the library I'll be glad to answer any questions," Christopher Ames said, and taking a calculated risk, he turned his back and proceeded down the hall to the book-lined room. Sputtering with anger, Ramsey followed close upon his heels. Once inside the room, the American, wanting the angry Earl to calm down enough to listen to what he had to say, procrastinated by offering the newcomer a glass of port or brandy.

"Damn your eyes, man! I came here thinking it was to a death bed, not to drink with you!" Ramsey shouted, moving threateningly toward the American.

Mr. Ames raised a glass of brandy to his lips, saying softly, "You told me once . . . upon another occasion . . . that I was the only man who had leveled you. Well, if you don't want me to be the only man to have done so twice, sit down like a gentleman and listen to me!"

For a few seconds the next move hung in the balance, but at last Ramsey seated himself, saying, "I didn't ride all this way to exchange blows with you. But if you are playing me for a fool, you'll answer to me this night!"

"No more a fool than you have made of yourself. If my faculties are reasonably intact I think you are more than a little in love with Sara Roche," Christopher Ames said. "And I have reason to believe she is not indifferent to you. But what you can have done to make such a muddle of things, I have no earthly idea."

"I would not have ridden like a madman through the night thinking her life in danger if there was not much in what you say," Ramsey admitted bitterly.

"Then why have you done nothing about it?" the American inquired mildly. "There is not a soul in London who isn't aware of your reputation for impulsiveness— and as a favorite with the fair sex. That is why I cannot for the life of me understand why you've behaved like a regular slow-top!"

"That, sir, is none of your business; nor is any of this, if I might add," the Earl said sarcastically. "You have yet to tell me why you brought me out here with an alarming falsehood. Surely, if you wished to discuss *my* private affairs with me, you could have done so at a more opportune time!"

"Since I'm about to become Sara's uncle-in-law, I made it my business. And it was not a complete falsehood; my fiancée, Augusta Roche, returned home from a party at Vauxhall Gardens a fortnight ago to find her niece out in the garden in her nightshift in the pouring rain and burning up with fever. Sara developed a severe pneumonia which only her youth and strong constitution pulled her through, for it was critical the first twenty-four hours!"

"Oh, my God!" Ramsey groaned. "My poor Sara! And it was all my fault!" He was on his feet, agitatedly pacing the room, his handsome face pale, his unusual eyes as dark as night.

"Have you had the measles lately?" Mr. Ames asked politely arching one eyebrow.

"What?" The Earl whirled toward him.

"Well, if you didn't have the measles in the past month or so, you can't lay her illness at your door, for it was measles which led to the pneumonia," the American announced, biting his lip to keep a smile from breaking through. "And if that's all that's been worrying you, why don't you march right into the drawing room and take over the rest of this affair yourself so I can go home to bed?"

"She wouldn't receive me—not after the way I've acted toward her," the Earl replied, sitting down wearily in a high-backed chair.

"Well, she can hardly run out of the house, you know. And since you are by far the larger and stronger of the two, I don't doubt you can manage to hold Sara's attention for a few minutes while you talk to her." The sight of the stony-faced countenance that met his gaze led Mr. Ames to the truth. "Oh, have you been making love to her? Well, that's nothing to act so shy about."

"You don't understand," Ramsey said in despair. "I . . . I tried to force my attentions on her! She will never want to see my face again!"

"Nonsense! You're a gentleman, even if your passions might have carried you away a bit. Talk to her, man!"

"No. No, she must abhor the sound of my very name." Ramsey continued.

"Did you kiss her?" Christopher Ames asked kindly.

"Yes. On two occasions." the dejected Earl responded without thinking.

"Did she slap your face?" Ames persisted.

"No," Ramsey answered.

"Did she scream for help?" the American prodded.

"Of course not!" the Earl rejoined in annoyance.

"Did she forbid you the house?" Christopher Ames continued. "Cancel your portrait sittings? Tell you she never wanted to see you again?"

"NO!" Ramsey shouted wrathfully.

"Then you don't have any problem, sapskull!" said the American in disgusted accents. "If you sit quietly without jumping up like a jack-in-the-box, I'll send her in to you, only she doesn't know you're here. So for God's sake, don't scare her!" and with this admonition, Mr. Ames walked jauntily back to the drawing room. He flung open the door, winked broadly at Augusta and announced to an astonished Sara that an urgent visitor awaited her in the library.

"But who can it be at this hour?" she inquired worriedly.

"That, you'll have to find out for yourself, my dear," Mr. Ames replied illusively. Sara left the room, having no idea who could be calling so late. Mr. Ames asked his beloved what she thought of setting Witherall up in a repertory theater in America as a business investment. Gussie thought it a capital idea!

Meanwhile Sara entered the dim library and peered around for a moment before seeing the tall figure standing in the shadow by the mantelpiece. Before her eyes had focused properly, a voice, strong but strangely husky, cried out to her.

"Please don't run away! Hear me out Sara, my darling!" Ramsey advanced to the center of the room.

"You!" Sara breathed, stunned. The candlelight highlighted the soft curve of her cheek and he saw her lips tremble, as her pupils dilated in alarm.

"Don't turn from me in revulsion, I beg of you. I would die before I did you any harm!" He took a hesitant step forward. Sara watched him come closer, his eyes taking on that burning amber glow that made her knees feel weak.

"Sara, my darling Sara, I know I have given you every reason to hold me in disgust, and cannot blame you for it. I have no excuse at all to offer, except that I love you and want you."

This was the moment Sara had feared. Her wanton response to his overtures must have given him every reason to think her a woman of easy virtue. She shrank from the feeling that he might be about to offer her *carte blanche*, yet knew that if he only raised his hand she would throw herself into his arms, regardless of his intentions. With a sinking feeling in her stomach Sara realized that if he wanted her, she was his. She *had* been his from that first kiss.

Ramsey saw her face soften, saw the way she looked at him, her misty blue-grey eyes shining. "Sara, oh Sara! Believe me, I want nothing more in life than to have you for my wife."

"Your wife!" Sara exclaimed.

"My love, do you think I would offer you anything less? I do truly love you," the Earl said quietly as he came across the room and stood looking down at her.

Sara blushed rosily. "I . . . I thought my behavior in the garden . . . would cause you to . . ." She trailed off in confusion before the warmth in his eyes.

Gently, Ramsey leaned down and kissed her mouth softly. With a sigh Sara surrendered to his embrace. He kissed her again, deeply and thoroughly, and she responded to him as she had that fateful night in the garden.

"Oh!" she said, pulling a little away from him, "what will you think of me, my lord?"

"Why, that you will make a *most* satisfactory wife, ma'am!" the Earl replied, pulling her close against his broad chest and kissing her again. "And my name, you know, is Edward," he added when he at last released her.

"Yes, Edward. Dearest, dearest, Edward!" Sara smiled, pulling his head down to hers, her eyes aglow with a light to equal the fire in his.

"We'll be married by special license tomorrow," he declared, "for I refuse to spend another night without you in my arms . . . or my bed."

"I think that is a very good idea, my love," Sara said, hugging him close and resting her cheek contentedly against his chest.

"I think I had better get that special license immediately," said the impulsive Lord Ramsey. "After all, if an Earl can be gotten out of bed for Cupid's errands, a Bishop can get up early too!" he laughed, kissing Sara on the nose. Then he kissed her eyelids, her face, her lips.

A voice came through the closed door. "Can you hurry it up, Ramsey, so we can get back to my place and get some sleep!" said Mr. Ames. "And in the morning we can both take care of those special licenses!"

"Yes, *Uncle*!" laughed the Earl, "but if you disturb us again I'll box your ears!" And he bent his head and kissed his beloved again.